YOU ARE

FIGHTING FA...

HOUSE OF HELL

STEVE JACKSON

Fighting Fantasy: dare you play them all?

1. The Warlock of Firetop Mountain
2. City of Thieves
3. The Citadel of Chaos
4. The Forest of Doom
5. House of Hell
6. The Port of Peril

HOUSE OF HELL

STEVE JACKSON

■SCHOLASTIC

Scholastic Children's Books
An imprint of Scholastic Ltd
Euston House, 24 Eversholt Street, London, NW1 1DB, UK
Registered office: Westfield Road, Southam, Warwickshire, CV47 0RA
SCHOLASTIC and associated logos are trademarks and/or
registered trademarks of Scholastic Inc.

First published in the UK by Penguin Group, 1984
This edition published in the UK by Scholastic Ltd, 2017

Text copyright © Steve Jackson, 1984
Cover illustration copyright © Robert Ball, 2017
Inside illustrations copyright © Vlado Krizan, 2017

The rights of Steve Jackson, Robert Ball and Vlado Krizan to be identified
as the author and illustrator of this work has been asserted by them.

Fighting Fantasy is a trademark owned by Steve Jackson
and Ian Livingstone, all rights reserved

ISBN 978 1407 18200 1

A CIP catalogue record for this book
is available from the British Library.

Printed by CPI Group (UK) Ltd, Croydon, CR0 4YY
Papers used by Scholastic Children's Books are made
from wood grown in sustainable forests.

1 3 5 7 9 10 8 6 4 2

www.scholastic.co.uk

CONTENTS

HOW WILL YOU START YOUR ADVENTURE?

8

BACKGROUND

11

THE HOUSE OF HELL

17

RULES AND EQUIPMENT

216

ADVENTURE SHEET

226

HOW WILL YOU START
YOUR ADVENTURE?

The book you hold in your hands is a gateway to another world – a world of dark magic, terrifying monsters, brooding castles, treacherous dungeons and untold danger, where a noble few defend against the myriad schemes of the forces of evil. Welcome to the world of **FIGHTING FANTASY!**

You are about to embark upon a thrilling fantasy adventure in which **YOU** are the hero! **YOU** decide which route to take, which dangers to risk and which creatures to fight. But be warned – it will also be **YOU** who has to live or die by the consequences of your actions.

Take heed, for success is by no means certain, and you may well fail in your mission on your first attempt. But have no fear, for with experience, skill and luck, each new attempt should bring you a step closer to your ultimate goal.

Prepare yourself, for when you turn the page you will enter an exciting, perilous **FIGHTING FANTASY** adventure where every choice is yours to make, an adventure in which **YOU ARE THE HERO!**

How would you like to begin your adventure?

IF YOU ARE NEW TO FIGHTING FANTASY...

It's a good idea to read through the rules which appear on pages 216-225 before you start.

IF YOU HAVE PLAYED FIGHTING FANTASY BEFORE...

You'll realize that to have any chance of success, you will need to discover your hero's attributes. You can create your own character by following the instructions on pages 216–225. Don't forget to enter your character's details on the Adventure Sheet which appears on page 226.

ALTERNATIVE DICE

If you do not have a pair of dice handy, dice rolls are printed throughout the book at the bottom of the pages. Flicking rapidly through the book and stopping on a page will give you a random dice roll. If you need to 'roll' only one die, read only the first printed die; if two, total the two dice symbols.

BACKGROUND

The rain spatters the windscreen relentlessly. You can see no more than a watery gloom as you strain forwards over the steering-wheel to see the road ahead. Although the wipers flap valiantly, they are fighting a losing battle, as the rain drives harder and harder. Your foot eases off the accelerator; the headlights struggle to light up the road.

Damn! You curse the white-haired old man who sent you off along this bumpy track. Probably he meant the *second* turning on the left – or even a *right* turning. The old fool. Perhaps this is his idea of a joke. After all, didn't you notice a mischievous glint in his eye? Something vaguely sinister?

But what sort of nonsense is this? So you've taken a wrong turn and got caught in a downpour in the night. The rain will ease off soon – it can't possibly keep up this deluge for long – and then you'll be able to ... *WATCH OUT!*

You spin the wheel frantically to the left to avoid the figure who, from nowhere, shows up in the head-lights. The car bumps and jolts as it bounces over the rocky roadside and thumps into a ditch.

You collect your thoughts. You are unhurt, but shaken. Then you remember what has happened. *The body!* You must have hit the figure which appeared; there was no way you could have avoided him. You spring out of the car, praying that he is still alive.

Your clothes soak up the rain as you hobble back to the road. In the darkness it is difficult to see anything. *But there is no sign of a body!*

You consider the situation. Are you certain that it was someone and not a trick of the light? Yes. You can remember the arms held up in fright as the car collided, and the look of anguish on his face. His *face!* There was something familiar about that face. A man you recognized. An old man; with white hair...

Your heart leaps: no, *impossible!* With a shiver of fear you race back to the car, jump inside, force the key into the ignition and twist it violently! The starter coughs, splutters and dies.

You hit the key again but this time a single shudder is all the engine can manage. You grasp the wheel with your hands and shake it desperately as if to force some life into the car. But the battery is dead. Your car is certainly not budging from the ditch tonight.

Your situation is hopeless. But now the plight of your car is paramount. Where can you get help? You passed a garage at Mingleford, but that was some twenty miles away.

As if in answer, a light appears in the distance. Someone has switched on a bedroom light. What a stroke of luck! It was at least fifteen miles back that you passed the last house and you happen to have broken down just a short distance from someone's home.

You button up your coat and open the door. From outside the car, you can see the building more clearly. Just ahead, on the left, a drive winds up to a large house. It is a good five minutes' walk away. And by the time you reach it, you will be drenched. But how else can you call the garage?

You can't afford to miss tomorrow's appointment. No, go you must. Anyway, you'll probably be able to dry off inside after phoning the garage.

You slam the door, turn up your collar and set off for the house. A flash of lightning lights it up clearly for you but, in your preoccupation with the rain, the warning from above is wasted on you. The house is old – very old – and in a shocking state of repair. The light in the window is flickering. Most likely an oil lamp – certainly not electric. And you don't notice a fact that might have turned you back anyway: there is no telephone line going to the house.

As you climb the steps to the front door, little do you realize what fate has in store for you.

Tonight is going to be a night to remember…

YOUR ADVENTURE AWAITS!

MAY YOUR STAMINA NEVER FAIL!

NOW TURN OVER...

The whole place seems to be deserted

You climb the creaking steps up to the front door and pause to catch your breath. Even though you ran all the way up the drive from the car, you are soaked through; your feet are particularly wet. Judging by the number of puddles you stepped into in the dark, the drive needs a small fortune spending on repairs. But under the porch, you are out of the storm, and you brush the rain from your clothes before turning towards the door.

The rain is still pelting down, but an eerie silence hangs in the air. No lights are on downstairs. You step back off the porch to check the upstairs window which attracted your attention earlier. Nothing. No lights. The whole place seems to be deserted. But then you remember the time – five minutes to midnight. Everyone in the house has probably gone to bed. An owl hoots in the distance and a shiver runs down your spine. The situation is a little scary. Here you are, in the middle of nowhere, at some strange, run-down old house about to wake up whoever lives inside, at midnight. They certainly won't be too pleased. But you have no choice if you are going to make your appointment tomorrow – you must reach a telephone to call for help. You step up to the front door.

From the left-hand side of the house, a dull glow catches your attention. A light has been turned on! You breathe a sigh of relief; at least someone is awake. You consider your options: there is an elaborate knocker in the middle of the door and a bell-pull hanging down to the right. Will you rap the door with the knocker (turn to **357**), pull the cord (turn to **275**), or creep round the house to investigate the light (turn to **289**)?

2

You may now proceed either by turning right and trying the door of the Shaitan room (turn to **200**), or by turning left and following the passage, which bears right past two rooms labelled Asmodeus and Eblis and then rejoins the landing (turn to **272**).

3

You grab the box and walk up to the mirror. You put your hand through again and pull it back. It seems safe enough. You step through ... just in the nick of time, for as you disappear into the mirror, you hear the door open behind you. You find you are in a small room behind the mirror. You decide to open the leather box. Inside is a Golden Key, which you put in your pocket. Now turn to **160**.

4

'Oh, a casual visitor, eh? Well, how do you like our dungeon, friend? Pleasant enough for you, is it? Having a good time? Bah! Into the cage with this miserable wretch!' The torturer's men tighten their grip on your wrists and frog-march you over to the left-hand wall. 'And we'll show our friend just how hospitable we are,' continues the torturer. 'What sort of accommodation would you like, friend? Do you want to spend the rest of your life crouching down or standing up?' The torturer's evil laugh resounds around the room. What will your answer be? Will you choose the tall cage (turn to **396**) or the box cage (turn to **201**)?

5

The bedroom has been prepared for you. The room is not large, but a huge mirror appears to double its size. Crisp white sheets have been folded back on the bed, and a warm fire burns in the fireplace. The door closes as the butler leaves the room and you walk over to the fire. Your situation is a little worrying. If you don't get going quickly, you will never make your appointment; but if it is true that there is no phone you can use, what else can you do? Maybe you should just hang your wet clothes in front of the fire and climb into bed (turn to **23**); or would you rather leave the room (turn to **59**)?

6

The door slowly opens and you hold yourself close to the wall. The man who enters is short and stocky and appears to be bent double. He is not armed. He peers into the room and scratches his head. Evidently he has heard something and is perplexed at finding nothing in the room. Will you step forward and announce yourself (turn to **367**) or keep hidden and hope he leaves (turn to **25**)?

7

The bell-push does not open a hidden panel, nor reveal any other means of escape. As you touch it, a loud bell starts ringing throughout the house! You bury your head in your hands. In a few moments you will be captured by the evil Earl of Drumer, his devil-worshippers and servants. And this time you will not escape...

8

You sit down in a solid, carved chair and look around. The reception hall is certainly not what you would have expected from the outside. It is elegantly decorated with rich tapestries and fine oak panels. A number of portraits line the walls. A sturdy sixteenth-century table is set against one wall. Will you wait for your host to arrive (turn to **277**), study the paintings (turn to **304**) or hunt for a telephone (turn to **238**)?

Resolve your battle with the Fire Sprites. They attack you one at a time:

	SKILL	STAMINA
First FIRE SPRITE	7	4
Second FIRE SPRITE	7	3

Each time they wound you, you risk the added danger of their flames touching you. You can either deduct 3 *STAMINA* points instead of the normal 2, or you may *Test your Luck* after each wound. A Lucky roll means you manage to put out the flame before it burns you (no *STAMINA* damage). An Unlucky roll means you lose 4 *STAMINA* points instead of 3. If you wish to *Escape* during the battle, turn to **218** – but the Sprites will get in a last hit as you leave. If you stay and fight them, turn to **375** if you win.

10

The Golden Key fits the lock and turns. The door opens to let you into another small room. The dust and cobwebs suggest that this room is very rarely used, and it certainly looks fairly uninteresting. But in the thick dust on the floor, you notice one footprint, then another. Someone has been in here recently! The footprints lead towards the right-hand wall, around the door. Behind a loose stone in the wall, you find what it was that this visitor came to hide – a large cast-iron key. You pick it up and examine it. It is heavy and fairly crudely made, and has the number 27 cast into it. You put this in your pocket. Nothing else of interest seems to be in the room, but you may add 2 *LUCK* points for this find. Now you must leave the chamber. Turn to **204**.

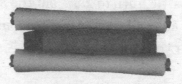

11

As you pull the door to, your ears catch the sound of another door opening. Someone is coming! You grab the handle and nip into the room, closing the door quietly behind you. You wait in the darkness. The door you heard closes and all goes quiet. Is someone lurking nearby? Turn to **385**.

12

You rummage through the box but there is nothing else hidden inside. The walls all feel solid except for the one on the left-hand side, adjacent to the secret entrance. You feel around and locate another secret door, but you cannot feel a catch. Perhaps the same password opens it. You try this, and the door starts to open slowly, revealing another room. You stare into this other room; it is almost an exact replica of the one in which you are standing! It is completely bare except for a table with a box resting on it. Fascinating! Do you wish to step into this other room (turn to **133**) or leave it and return through your original door to go upstairs (turn to **293**)?

13

You step into the room and close the door behind you. The room is empty and you heave a sigh of relief, falling back against the door to catch your breath. Will you rest in the room (turn to **372**) or try the window for a means of escape (turn to **107**)?

14

The smell from within the room catches you off balance and stops you dead in your tracks. The room itself is unexciting, with bare rocky walls and floor. But strewn around the floor are the headless bodies of five goats. Standing over the goats, feeding ravenously on them, are three huge Great Danes! As you enter the room, they turn towards you, angry at having their meal interrupted. Their mouths curl back and they snarl. The nearest dog leaps towards you and you must fight it:

GREAT DANE   *SKILL 7*   *STAMINA 5*

If you defeat the dog, turn to **94**.

15

You tug at the handle, but the door is locked. If you have a key, turn to **212**. If you do not have a key, turn to **47**.

16

'A friend of the Master?' snarls the torturer. 'I have not seen you before. And I know *all* the Master's friends.' You tell him that you are new to this house, and that is why you are wandering about, lost. The torturer is not convinced by your story, but cannot risk harming one of the Master's friends. 'I'll tell you what I'll do,' he announces. '*I* don't believe you. But I'll give you a chance. If you can convince me that you are one of the Master's friends, I'll let you go. But first you'll have to pass a little test. Tie our friend down, lads!' The torturer's assistants bundle you off to the middle of the room and tie you on to the rack. Turn to **381**.

17

The two men snatch the box from you. One of them pulls out a dagger! He snarls and lunges at you with it. Although you leap out of the way, you must add 2 *FEAR* points for the fright. The other man grabs his friend's wrist. 'Do not waste your time. Hide the box for the Master and I will deal with our visitor!' The man with the dagger grunts in agreement and backs towards the door. As he leaves the room, the other advances. Resolve your fight with him:

THE MASTER'S SERVANT   *SKILL 8*   *STAMINA 9*

If you defeat him, you may leave the room (turn to **131**).

18

He tells you that there are all sorts of secrets in the cellars. '...And some of them I just couldn't tell you. It would be more than my life's worth. For the Master would punish me. And I wouldn't like that.' Needless to say, this only makes you more intrigued. But he will not be pressed on the subject. If you have a weapon, you may draw it out and threaten the Hunchback (turn to **191**). If you have any brandy, you may offer him a drink (turn to **93**). If you have neither of these, turn to **347**.

19

You search the room, while the old woman threatens you from her bed. You recognize some of the plants, as most of them are common house-plants. The woman's voice grows frantic as you poke around in a herb garden by the window. A thought dawns on you and you turn to her, threatening to destroy her plants unless she is able to give you the information you require. She shrieks at the thought of you harming her plants and agrees. What will you ask her:

How to find the man in grey?	Turn to **388**
About the secret rooms in the house?	Turn to **321**
What tonight's 'festivities' are?	Turn to **283**

20

As his slaves fall dead on the floor, the Vampire rises to his feet, ready to finish you off. You quickly hold up your garlic and he stands his ground. But what can you do now? You may either try the other door (turn to **270**) or head back for the entrance door (turn to **90**).

21

You walk along the passageway. Do you want to try the door on the left (turn to **259**) or the door on the right (turn to **118**)?

22

'Lies!' he snarls, in response to your explanation. 'You are like all the others in this house. I must destroy you all!' Shouting this warning, he leaps towards you. Turn to **271**.

23

The bed is warm and comfortable and you soon drift off to sleep. Strange and disturbing thoughts drift through your mind and you wake suddenly in a cold sweat. A noise has disturbed you and you realize that it was the sound of the door closing. You look around the room and notice a glass containing a clear liquid by the side of your bed. *Someone has brought you a bedtime drink!* You spring out of bed and try the door, but it is locked. Do you wish to swallow the drink that has been brought for you (turn to **45**) or will you try to break down the door (turn to **128**)?

24

The door opens and you find yourself in a small room. There is another door leading off the room. But in front of you is a strange sight which catches your attention. A shimmering haze seems to be hanging on the wall, almost like a curtain of sparkling water. You step up to investigate and gingerly hold out your finger to touch it. Your finger passes right through! Plucking up your courage, you poke your head into the haze. On the other side, you realize what has happened. Your head has emerged through a large mirror into a reception room. On the wall opposite is a huge mural of a country scene and standing in the middle of the room are a table and six chairs. The sound of voices outside the door startles you and you draw your head back. Will you wait until the way is clear and step through the mirror (turn to **349**), try the other door in this little room behind the mirror (turn to **294**) or will you instead go back to the stairs and follow them down (turn to **216**)?

25

The little man stares once more into the room, shrugs his shoulders and leaves, closing the door behind him. You are alone again. After waiting a few minutes, you decide to leave the room. Turn to **116**.

26

There is another door a couple of metres up the landing on the left. This is the door to the Mephisto room. If you wish to enter, turn to **298**. Otherwise you may pass it and head towards two doors in the corner of the landing (turn to **287**).

27

You draw back the curtains and peer outside. The light in the room makes it difficult to see, so you pull the curtains behind you. With your face pressed against the bars, you look through the window. There is a rumble of thunder in the distance and the rain is still beating down, making it difficult to see anything. A fork of lightning flashes down from the sky and lights up a sight which makes you cry out loud! Outside your window, dripping wet and swaying in the wind, is a ghastly face! A long-dead figure, hanging in a noose, is staring at you with lifeless eyes. You step back and fling the curtains shut to hide the horrendous sight. The face is familiar. *The old man in the village!* You must add 3 *FEAR* points. What will you do now? Will you dive into bed and sleep through the night (turn to **231**) or run out on to the landing (turn to **121**)?

28

The Earl of Drumer is the last survivor of his family. His estate stretches for miles around the house. At one time the estate was prosperous, with many tenant farmers cultivating his land and providing a healthy income for his family. But things started to change. His sister died at the age of thirty-two under mysterious circumstances. She was found dead in a clearing in the woods with strange marks on her neck. News travelled fast, and the ignorant peasants started muttering about witchcraft and black magic. In their eyes, the house was cursed. Pure superstitious nonsense, of course, but gradually the farmers moved to new pastures, avoiding the estate.

By now you have finished your meal. Franklins returns to offer you fruit, cheese, coffee and brandy. Will you take:

Fruit, coffee and brandy?	Turn to **224**
Cheese, coffee and brandy?	Turn to **74**
Just cheese arid coffee?	Turn to **319**

29

As the Ghoul slumps to the floor, it falls against a rack of pans hanging on the wall. The pans clatter to the floor; the noise is deafening! Have you been heard? Turn to **254** to find out.

30

Resolve your battle with the Earl of Drumer. If you are using the Kris knife, add 3 points to your *SKILL* during the fight:

THE EARL OF DRUMER   *SKILL* 9   *STAMINA* 10

If you win, turn to **288**.

31

As you scramble for the door, you slip in a pool of goat's blood and slither on to the floor. The dogs seize their chance and spring on top of you. Turn to **78** and fight the dogs. But because you are at a disadvantage, having fallen over, you must deduct 2 from your Attack Strength for the first four Attack Rounds.

32

You draw your weapon and advance. The man jumps back at the sight of it, but you stride closer. As you prepare to strike, a sly smile spreads across his face. Turn to **326**.

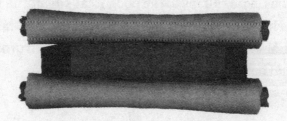

33

A short distance further along the balcony you arrive at a door with Azazel written on the name-plate. If you wish to try this door, turn to **358**. If you would prefer to continue, turning to the left and following the landing, turn to **229**.

34

How good are your powers of persuasion? Throw two dice and compare the total with your *SKILL* score. If you roll a number equal to or less than your *SKILL* score, turn to **177**. If you roll a number greater than your *SKILL* score, turn to **22**.

35

Your eyes light up as the lid falls back. The box is lined with red velvet and there in the middle is a pearl-handled dagger. Its silver blade is wavy but it is finely polished and razor-sharp. An inscription in the wooden top reads:

The Kris Knife
A blade fashioned for the glorification and pleasure of the Demons of Hellfire – our true Masters. To be used only by Initiates. Never to be wielded in the presence of the Masters.

A sense of awe fills you as you pick up the knife. You turn it over tenderly in your hands and then place it in your pocket. For this find you may add 3 *LUCK* points. Now you must decide what to do next. Will you leave the way you entered and climb the stairs to the ground floor (turn to **293**) or will you search the room thoroughly first (turn to **12**)?

36

You may now leave the food store. Will you try the door opposite (turn to **305**) or retrace your steps along the passageway (turn to **366**)?

37

You study the portrait of 'The Duke of Brewster: 1763-1828'. A rather elegant sort of chap, you think as you stare at him. But suddenly you jump back! You could swear you saw his eyes *move! A* moment later, your suspicions are confirmed. His eyes are definitely moving, directing your attention towards one of the doors in the hall. What is happening? Your car breaks down and suddenly you are in an elegantly decorated derelict house, with moving portraits! Will you sit back in the chair and wait for your host to return (turn to **277**) or try the handle on the door that the portrait is looking at (turn to **391**)? You may, if you wish, look at another painting by turning to **250**.

38

The first letter Orville gives you is D. You must start writing straight away, or you will have to deduct 1 point from your *STAMINA* score as Dirk tightens the rack. When you are ready, turn to **352**.

39

With a superhuman effort, you beat down the hypnotic power of the eye and slam the book shut. Replacing it on the shelf, you rub your eyes. Although a little dazed, you are safe. But you decide to leave this room without delay. Turn to **54**.

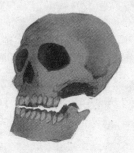

40

The box rattles when you touch it. There is something solid inside. You undo the catch and open the lid. Inside you find a small key. You try the key in the door and it fits! The key turns and unlocks the door, allowing you to leave the room. You find you are in the corner of the landing, and there is an unmarked door to your left. If you wish to go through it, turn to **86**. Straight ahead, you can see the main staircase leading downwards. If you wish to go this way, turn to **193**.

Inside, partly dressed in tattered clothes, are two skeletons

41

Starting at the far end, you examine the cupboards. You open the first door and find it is a wardrobe with dresses and blouses hanging inside. You open the second door – and spring backwards in fright! For inside, partly dressed in tattered clothes, are two SKELETONS. Having disturbed them by opening the door, they are coming to life before your eyes and advancing to attack! You must add 2 *FEAR* points for the fright and then fight them, one at a time:

	SKILL	STAMINA
First SKELETON	6	6
Second SKELETON	7	6

If you defeat the Skeletons, you may either look around the room (turn to **338**) or leave (turn to **243**).

42

The hallway narrows by the stairs and widens again further on. You may turn left here (turn to **316**), or follow the hallway round to the right and try the first door on the right (turn to **217**).

43

Starting at the far end, you examine the cupboards. You open the first door and find it is a wardrobe with dresses and blouses hanging inside. You open the second door – and spring backwards in fright! For inside, partly dressed in tattered clothes, are two SKELETONS. Having disturbed them by opening the door, they are coming to life before your eyes and advancing to attack! You must add 2 *FEAR* points for the shock and you must now fight them, one at a time:

	SKILL	STAMINA
First SKELETON	6	6
Second SKELETON	7	6

If you defeat the Skeletons, you may look through the cupboards before you leave. Turn to **368**.

44

The door is not locked. You open it cautiously and poke your head inside. You have found a food store of some kind; the room is lined with shelves with various foodstuffs on them. Bread, dried meats, cheese, fruit, dried fish, wine (red and white) and cakes are all neatly stacked on the shelves. If you need to restore some of your *STAMINA,* you may choose any of these to eat. Note which you take, then turn to **227**. If you would rather not risk taking any of them, turn instead to **36**.

45

The liquid has a slightly sweet taste, like water with a spoonful of sugar dissolved in it. But your mouth is dry from your sleep and you drink it down. You lie back, thinking about your visitor. You decide it was probably Franklins, the butler. It was nice of him to bring you a drink, but why has he locked the door? Again, you start to feel tired, and you curl up on the bed. Your head starts to swim and the room spins round. Too late, you realize that you have been drugged! Although you try your best to fight the feeling, it is no use. Consciousness fades... Turn to **173**.

46

Do you have any garlic with you? If so, turn to **361**. If you have a gold ring edged with rubies, turn to **135**. If you have both of these, you may choose to use either. If you have neither, choose another weapon and turn to **32**.

47

Where would you like to go next? The Shaitan room at the end of the passage (turn to **200**), the Mammon room opposite (turn to **123**), or would you rather turn back down the passageway and follow the landing round (turn to **272**)?

48

You step into the small room. Glancing round to make sure you are safe, you walk up to the table. The rest of the room is bare, except for the table and the box which rests on it. Could this be the one you are looking for? It is a handsome rectangular box made of wood with brass fastenings. It looks like a case for a pair of duelling pistols. You undo the catch and flip back the lid. Turn to **35**.

49

You have a choice of three doors here. Will you go through the door at the end of the passageway (turn to **195**), try the door on the left (turn to **307**) or try the door on the right (turn to **217**)?

50

Your groping hand touches a piece of wood. You feel it and find that it is a length of branch about the size of a baseball bat. If you use this in a fight, it will count as a WEAPON (add 3 *SKILL* points). Now you must return to the matter of your visitor. Will you attack as soon as the door opens (turn to **183**) or will you keep the stick hidden and wait to see what comes through the door (turn to **263**)?

51

If you wish to look for secret doorways, turn to **276**. Otherwise return to the last reference and choose again.

52

The Hell Demon steps forward and slashes at you with its claws, catching your arm with such force that it breaks. You shriek and clutch your injured arm, now useless in the battle. But your agony will be short-lived. For nothing you can do will defeat this unearthly creature. The battle – and your life – will shortly come to an end. . .

53

You try to spring aside, but the chair is too quick for you. It smacks into your shin, causing you to howl in pain. Lose 2 *STAMINA* points and also add 1 *FEAR* point for the unnerving experience. You had better leave the room before the POLTERGEIST injures you more seriously! Turn to **2**.

He is not bent double at all – he is a HUNCHBACK!

54

There are two doors leading out of the study. Did you enter from the drawing-room? If so, you can leave through the other door (turn to **247**). If you entered from the hallway, you may now leave through the other door by turning to **353**.

55

'Tonight?' she croaks. 'Let's see. Ah yes, there is a ceremony tonight. Brother Samuelson – no, I think it's Isaacson – will be receiving the Master's blessing. If I were you I'd stay well away from the ceremony, though. They don't like onlookers.' She coughs a little and her eyes close, as if the strain of talking was too much for her. You consider her words and leave her in peace, heading for the door. Turn to **159**.

56

As the fight starts, you can see that he is not bent double at all – he is a HUNCHBACK! Now resolve your battle with him:

HUNCHBACK   *SKILL 7*   *STAMINA 7*

After three Attack Rounds, turn to **72**.

57

'Come, come, Orville. Let's have another.' Orville thinks again and this time says 'K!' Write your answer quickly, or deduct another *STAMINA* point. Turn to **333**.

58

The hallway widens. You walk across to another hallway and continue in the direction you were walking until you reach two doors opposite each other. Will you try the door on the right (turn to **118**) or the door on the left (turn to **323**)?

59

The door is locked! It seems that your hosts certainly don't want you prowling around the house. Do you want to try to break down the door (turn to **79**), or climb into bed (turn to **23**)? If you prefer, you could pretend to go to bed, switch out the light and wait to see what happens (turn to **63**).

60

There seems to be no other way out of the passage. Even the panel through which you entered has now closed up. A bell-push is set in the wall and, hoping that this will reveal some way out, you push it. Turn to **7**.

61

There is nothing unusual under the stairs, although some of the bricks in the wall look as if they have been replaced recently. You may either look in the bats' corner (turn to **165**), along the back wall (turn to **356**) or climb the stairs to the door above (turn to **293**).

62

The collection contains many invaluable first editions and obscure works in strange languages. The Earl of Drumer has a disturbingly large collection of books on black magic and many volumes on hypnotism. Do you want to look at any of them? If so, will you choose a book on Black Magic (turn to **156**) or a book on Hypnotism (turn to **384**)?

63

You wait in the darkness. Apart from the rain driving against the window, the house is silent. How long will you have to wait before someone appears? All night? The thought of sitting in the darkness all night makes you a little uneasy and you must add 1 *FEAR* point. But then you hear a shuffling noise in the corridor outside your room. Turn to **158**.

64

The Fire Sprites follow you as you back towards the window. Pretending to be terrified, you make for one of the plant-pot stands and attempt to hide behind it. But when the Sprites are near enough, you strike! Grabbing the large plant-pot on top of the stand, you hurl the contents over the little creatures! The soil covers them and douses their flames; in an instant they have disappeared. Turn now to **375**.

65

'The man in grey? Who is he? You'll have to forgive me, stranger. As you can imagine, it is some time since I wandered round the house. I don't even know who is here any more. Except, of course, the Earl and his manservant, Franklins. But a man in grey... Wait! I know who he might be! In the cellars, a man is being held captive in a room opposite the food store. Could this be the man in grey? I thought he wore white. Perhaps he's a little dirtier now.' Her voice fades, as if the conversation was too much of a strain for her. You decide to leave her and head for the door. Turn to **159**.

66

You hold up your pentacle before them and command them to step back to allow you to pass. Gasps come from the crowd as they see the pentacle. But its power cannot be denied. They watch powerlessly as you back down the other passageway and open the door at the end. Turn to **232**.

67

The dagger is no use to you in this predicament; but what about the flask of liquid? You hold it up and study the contents. The swirling black liquid is thick and oily. Rainbow patterns and reflections play tricks on your eyes. You could swear you were looking straight into a pair of dark eyes inside the flask! But you swirl the liquid once more and the image disappears. You imagine that you have nothing to lose by opening the flask, so you remove the stopper. What happens next is instantaneous! As soon as the stopper leaves the neck of the flask, the liquid turns into a billowing black smoke, which hisses out and fills the room. The room goes black instantly. Just as quickly, the smoke is sucked back into the flask and the stopper reappears in position. All is as before, with one exception. You are no longer in the room! Your body has been sucked into the flask by the NANKA – a type of Evil Genie – living inside it. Your adventure ends here.

68

The younger man turns to the older one and angrily says, 'The Master's teachings are not for the faint-hearted. You know of his power and his promises to us all. Perhaps you are no longer strong enough to stay with us.' The older man turns away, towards the window. He is hiding the look on his face, which is one of nervousness and fear. He realizes that he has said the wrong thing. 'No,' he stammers, 'I'll be all right. Just a momentary weakness. Come, let us get on with the preparations.' Together the two men leave the kitchen, blowing out the candles on the way. You wonder what they were talking about. Now you must choose your next move. Will you try the kitchen door to see whether you can sneak inside (turn to **306**) or go back round to the front and knock on the door (turn to **357**)?

69

You step inside and close the door quietly behind you. A soft click comes from the lock. As you step forward, a voice greets you. You look around but you can see no one! The voice continues: 'So! Our visitor is inquisitive, eh? Or are you trying to leave the house? Perhaps our hospitality is not to your liking. Maybe you would like to see some more – shall we say – *amusements?*' The eerie voice makes you nervous. Add 1 *FEAR* point. Do you wish to stay and talk to the voice (turn to **291**) or will you make a hasty exit back through the door (turn to **120**)?

70

You walk over slowly and reach out for the sheet. It now hangs in the air well above the box it was covering. You grip it in your hand and tug it downwards. It snaps, confirming your suspicions. The sheet was being pulled by a thin strand of string. You breathe a sigh of relief (you may deduct the *FEAR* point you had just taken). But who, or what, was pulling the sheet? You decide not to wait to find out. Leave the room by turning to **329**.

71

You open the door and cast your eyes over the room inside. The floor is dusty and the rocky walls are bare. A rough wooden table and chair are placed against one wall. Sitting at the table is a worried-looking man wearing a white robe. A goat's head mask lies on the table. 'Hello,' he says, nervously. 'All hail the Master, I am ready to repent. How is the ceremony progressing? Er, um, is it my turn yet?' Then he leans forward and whispers to you: '*I am not a poor man. Help me to escape from this house and you will be generously rewarded.*' What do you make of all this? Will you tell him the truth about yourself (turn to **214**), or will you remain emotionless and let him continue (turn to **334**)?

72

Have you come across this Hunchback before? If so, turn to **138**. If not, turn to **164**.

73

To enter the room, she passes right through the door! You, of course, must use more traditional methods; you turn the handle and walk into the Apollyon room. It is an elegant bedroom. Fine floor-length curtains hang along one wall. An enormous bed with lace coverings is against another wall; and opposite stands a beautiful dressing-table with a huge mirror. The woman hovers in the centre of the room and bids you to sit down on the bed. 'Your coming here has been no accident,' she starts. 'And I must warn you of the terrible dangers you will face here. This house is ruled by the *Master*, a powerful Black Priest of the Night, named Kelnor, Earl of Drumer. I would guess that you are to be offered to the Demons of Hellfire, if you survive that long. Yesterday they trapped a girl, a pretty young district nurse who happened to call. She is to be offered tonight. *I cannot let this devilry continue!* There must be some way it can be stopped! If you can find the Kris knife, you might defeat Kelnor, for this weapon is his only weakness. Please help me! You will probably find it in. . . *No!* Quick! We are discovered. I can hear the Hounds. Go! Leave this room!' You stand up. She was right! You can hear barking getting rapidly closer. She motions to you, pointing at the door. You run to the door and peer outside. Nothing. The barking gets louder and you turn back towards the Ghost, who seems to be struggling with something. She is involved in a fight with two huge ghostly Great Danes which are snapping and clawing at her. You take a step forwards, but it is hopeless. You cannot help, as you cannot even touch the beasts. And your help would have been very welcome, because the dogs are much too powerful for her. She is weakening and, as she does so, her image fades. Moments later she disappears completely. Satisfied that their job has been done, the two Great Danes disappear also. You are alone. Now what will *you* do? Do you want to help her as she asked (turn to **257**), or would you rather just escape from the house (turn to **346**)?

74

You finish off your meal. The Earl rises to his feet, saying: 'Our conversation has been most enjoyable, but now you must be very tired. Franklins will show you to your room. Let us retire.' You stand up. He's right, you *are* tired, and it is well past midnight. You stumble and reach out to steady yourself against the table. Phew! You didn't realize you were *that* tired. Or have you had a little too much to drink? Your head is spinning; and the voice of your host becomes part of a background noise which is getting louder and louder in your ears. Eventually you collapse to the ground and lose consciousness... Turn to **173**.

75

'Escape from this house?' he laughs. 'Would that we could both escape from this place! I will find my own way out, as I have a mission to complete before I leave. You may choose your own escape-route, though none is safe. The front door is at the foot of the staircase. As you no doubt entered that way, you could try leaving by it; or perhaps you could leap from the window? Unfortunately most of them are barred. There is a secret passageway through the cellar which leads outside, but the chances of finding it are slim. Anyway, my thanks for releasing me. We will part company here.' The man peers round the door to check the passageway, then leaves the room. You may either leave after him (turn to **378**) or walk over to the table and boxes to examine them (turn to **213**).

76

Orville has been practising his next letter and blurts it out excitedly. S is his choice. Write immediately or lose a *STAMINA* point, then turn to **315**.

77

You try the doorknob, but it will not move! You are locked in the room. A shiver of anxiety comes over you. Add 1 *FEAR* point. Unless you can find a way out, you are trapped. Perhaps there may be a clue in the box on the mantelpiece. Turn to **40**.

78

Resolve your fight. The dogs attack one at a time:

	SKILL	STAMINA
Second GREAT DANE	6	6
Third GREAT DANE	6	5

If you defeat both of them, turn to **383**.

79

Roll two dice and compare the total with your *SKILL* score. If it is higher than your *SKILL* score (use your *Initial SKILL* score), turn to **106**. If it is equal to or lower than your *SKILL* score, turn to **128**.

80

You look around the chamber. Another passageway leads from the chamber. If you choose your moment carefully, you may be able to reach it without being noticed. Will you move quietly along the wall towards it (turn to **187**) or will you instead watch the proceedings (turn to **314**)?

81

In a drawer underneath the bench you find a few ornate letter-openers. Perhaps they are someone's collection?

You are particularly interested because they are strong and dagger-like. In fact they could easily make dangerous weapons. You may take one of them if you wish, and as a WEAPON it will allow your *SKILL* score to increase to its *Initial* value if you use it in a fight. Now turn to **385**.

82

There is no way you will find of opening the door, as it will only open and shut at the command of the Earl of Drumer. You are now his prisoner and will remain trapped for the rest of your life within these four walls.

83

Various items of crockery, cutlery and food are kept in the storeroom, including a sharp meat-knife, which you might like to hide under your coat to use as a WEAPON in the future. This sharp knife will allow you to add 3 *SKILL* points in a fight. On one shelf you find several cloves of garlic which you may also take. There is also an unlabelled bottle of white liquid on another shelf. If you wish to drink the liquid, turn to **362**. If you would prefer to ignore the liquid and try the door at the back of the storeroom, turn to **255**. Your only other alternative is to leave by the door you entered and return to the landing (turn to **233**).

Their flaming bodies burn with the vigour of the fire from which they arose

84

There is nothing special about this food. Turn to **36**.

85

The little carving moves to reveal a button set in the mantelpiece behind it. You consider whether or not to press the button. As you are deep in thought, you do not notice what is happening to the fire. In the grate, the fire has come back to life! Strong flames are licking the chimney and considerable heat is being given off. You feel the heat and step backwards. As you do so, two small figures leap from the fire and face you. These FIRE SPRITES are small – they come up to your knees – but their flaming bodies burn with the vigour of the fire from which they arose. They hover in the air just above the carpet; for if they touch anything, it bursts into flame. Do you wish to fight these creatures (turn to **9**) or will you try another approach (turn to **145**)?

86

The door opens into a narrow passageway which ends at a window. There is a door half-way along the left-hand side, and a sign on the door identifies it as the Diabolus room. If you wish to try this door, turn to **13**. If you wish to investigate the window instead, turn to **110**. If you're not keen to do either and would prefer to go back through the door and continue along the landing, turn to **193**.

87

The door bursts open! Two white-robed men enter. At least, you *presume* they are men, but their faces are hidden behind masks made out of goats' heads. They carry knives and leap forward to attack; one attacks you and the other attacks your comrade. Resolve your own fight first:

DEVIL-WORSHIPPER   *SKILL 8*   *STAMINA 7*

If you defeat him, turn to **178**.

88

She curses. 'Damn you, stranger,' she hisses. 'All right then, I will answer your question.' Which question did you ask her?

How to find the man in grey?	Turn to **65**
About the secret rooms in the house?	Turn to **295**
What tonight's 'festivities' are?	Turn to **55**

89

You follow the stairs downwards. Running across the bottom is a passageway. You turn right and follow it until you reach a dead end with two doors facing each other on opposite sides of the wall. Will you try the door on the left (turn to **305**), the door on the right (turn to **44**) or will you turn around and head back the way you came (turn to **366**)?

90

You fling your garlic at the Vampire and dash for the door. He shrieks as he tries to brush it off, but this will at least keep him occupied for a few moments more. However, your luck is out. The door is locked! And the Vampire is now striding towards you, his eyes firmly fixed on yours. Do you have a gold ring edged with rubies? If so, turn to **135**. Otherwise, turn to **326**.

91

Further up the passage is another door in the right-hand wall. If you wish to try this door, turn to **112**. If you want to pass it and continue along the corridor, turn to **393**.

92

The door opens on to a dark landing. A flight of stairs arrives at this landing and continues downwards. Will you follow the stairs down (turn to **216**) or would you rather close the door and step back through the mirror (turn to **349**)?

93

His eyes light up at the sight of the brandy. You pour a little into the cap of the hip-flask and pass it to him. He gulps it down and licks his lips. After two more capfuls, he is definitely slurring his speech. You tell him that you have heard of secret passageways in the cellar and that you would be very interested in being shown around by someone as knowledgeable as he is. Your flattery, and the brandy, have their desired effect. Proudly he tells you all about his cellars – much more than he should. 'Of course, not everyone can get round these cellars,' he boasts. 'You've got to know the password to get through some of the secret doors. And the Master keeps changing the password to protect his secrets. In fact only yesterday he changed the password from Pravemi to. . . Oh, what was it now? It's on the tip of my tongue. Ach, I should remember it because it is like the name of the house, but *mixed up! My mind's mixed up!* It must be you and your brandy!' He steps back, realizing that he's said enough. You try asking him more, but he will not speak. Instead he turns towards the door in the left-hand wall and leaves you, pointing down the passageway and mumbling something about upstairs. Turn to **393** to follow the passageway or **166** to look around.

94

The other two Great Danes snarl and advance towards you. If you wish to fight them, turn to **78**. If you wish to escape, you must *Test your Luck*. If you are Lucky, turn to **240**. If you are Unlucky, turn to **31**.

95

The door opens wide and the older man peers out at you before inviting you in. The two men listen as you tell them of your accident. 'Well, that is a stroke of bad luck,' says the older man, 'but I dare say Franklins will be able to help. Go and fetch him, Brother William.' At the mention of his name, the younger man glares at his companion, but nevertheless leaves the kitchen. You ask your host what sort of place this is and whether he and Brother William are members of a religious group. 'Something like that,' he replies. 'In fact you have arrived at an awkward time. For tonight...' he hesitates nervously, 'tonight is...' His sentence is interrupted by the arrival of Brother William and a tall man dressed in a black suit with long tails. You explain your arrival to Franklins. 'We do not welcome visitors here,' says Franklins solemnly, 'but I will introduce you to the master of the house who will decide whether we can help. Follow me.' He leads you out through the kitchen along a hallway to a reception hall and points to a seat. 'Wait here while I tell the Earl,' he orders, then he disappears through a doorway. Turn to **8**.

96

The Earl rings for his butler, who appears in the room immediately. 'Franklins, our guest has decided not to eat. Our hospitality has been refused. Deal with the situation!' The butler nods and touches a button on the back of your chair. Clasps appear from the arms and snap closed across your wrists, holding you in place! You squirm to free yourself, but you cannot break their grip. Meanwhile, the butler has pulled a handkerchief out of his pocket and is shaking a pungent liquid into it from a glass bottle. You cannot avoid it as he holds the cloth over your mouth. *Chloroform!* You begin to lose consciousness... Turn to **173**.

97

You try the handle without success. The door is firmly locked and you decide to follow the hallway instead. Where the hallway widens, you may either turn left (turn to **316**) or follow the hallway round to the right and try the door immediately on the right (turn to **217**).

98

You open the door cautiously at first, but all you can see is darkness, so you swing it wide open. *Aaaiieeeee!* You scream out loud as a body tumbles forward on top of you! The body is that of an old man and, judging by the expression on his face, his death was not a pleasant one. You must add 3 *FEAR* points. You panic and run off round the landing. Turn to **374**.

99

As the lid falls back, your eyes light up. Inside the box is a pearl-handled dagger! You reach down and pick up the dagger, admiring its workmanship. But the dagger was not the only thing in the box. Lying underneath it is a flask, which contains a black liquid. You can take this with you if you wish. You slide the dagger into your pocket and turn towards the door. But your heart sinks as the door slams shut in front of you! You try to open it, but there is no handle. Will you search the room for a way of opening the door (turn to **82**) or will you see whether the dagger or the flask of liquid can help (turn to **67**)?

100

You shut the secret compartment and nip quickly behind the curtains. Moments later the door opens and your hear footsteps coming into the room. Two men enter, in the middle of a heated discussion. Although you can hear only part of the conversation, they are talking about a ceremony which involves a human sacrifice! You swallow hard and hope that you are not likely to get involved in it; but add 1 *FEAR* point for the thought. You keep motionless behind the curtains. Sure enough, the men walk up to the table. You hear a faint click and a drawer slides open. Then the men turn and leave the room. When it is safe, you come out of your hiding-place and check the compartment. They have taken the leather box with them. Will you now leave through the door (turn to **131**) or through the mirror (turn to **160**)?

101

In the nick of time, you spring aside as the chair speeds past you and crashes into the wall behind. You escape injury, but you must add 1 *FEAR* point. You had better now leave the room before the POLTERGEIST inside does you some real damage! Turn to **2**.

102

The passageway is narrow and only the faintest glow lights your way. After a short distance you come to a staircase which leads downwards. Slowly and cautiously you go down the stairs. After a dozen or so steps, you reach another landing. The stairs continue downwards at the landing and you may either follow them down (turn to **216**), or you may try a door in the wall of the landing (turn to **24**).

103

You open the door slowly and carefully. The room you enter is a bedroom which looks as though it is waiting for someone to come in and go to bed! The sheets are folded back, the fire in the fireplace is warm but dying. On the bedside table a candle is burning and next to it is a silver tray with a bedtime snack on it. Velvet curtains are pulled across the window, and along the left-hand wall are fitted-cupboards. The overall picture is quite cosy. Will you enter the room and investigate the bedside table (turn to **163**) or the cupboards (turn to **41**), or are you a little suspicious of the apparent tranquillity of this room and would prefer to leave (turn to **243**)?

104

You feel a stab of pain in your back. You reach out to grip the wound and blood oozes through your fingers! Even though his master is dead, Franklins will fight on! You turn round to face the butler before he can attack again with his knife. Deduct 4 *STAMINA* points and turn to **180**.

105

'Defeat the Master, eh?' he says, watching you carefully. 'My word, our friend certainly cannot be said to have modest ambitions! You will never defeat the Master, for he has only one weakness. He may only be killed with the Kris knife, and that is hidden in a room with a secret entrance. I know only that the room is downstairs and that you will need a password to open it. But I do not know what the password is. Old Mordana knew the password, but she died some time ago. If you know what's best for you, you will leave while you can.' You ask him whether the two of you should leave together, but he shakes his head. 'I cannot leave here without seeking my revenge – or dying in the attempt. I must leave you now.' He checks the passageway, then nips out. Will you follow him (turn to **378**) or will you first check the table and the boxes (turn to **213**)?

106

You charge at the door with your shoulder. The door shudders but holds firm and you are left nursing an aching shoulder. Deduct 2 *STAMINA* points. You realize that the door is made of solid wood and you are unlikely to break it open without doing yourself an injury. Turn to **158**.

107

You walk over to the curtains and part them slowly. Outside, the storm is still raging. Thunder rolls across the sky and rain rattles against the window. The window is barred. There is no way out here. Turn to **168**.

108

The hallway widens. To your left, there is a passage with two doors facing each other across it. To go this way, turn to **21**. If you don't want to go this way, you can walk on a couple of metres and turn right into a passageway which runs past two doors facing each other and ends at another door. To go this way, turn to **49**.

109

Can you defeat the demon which now stands before you? If not, it will certainly kill you. But you have with you the Kris knife, the only weapon which will harm the creature. You may add 6 points to your *SKILL* score while using this weapon. Now resolve this battle:

HELL DEMON   *SKILL 14*   *STAMINA 12*

If you win the fight, turn to **400**.

110

Curtains are drawn across the window, and you approach cautiously. You gingerly pat the folds in the curtain and are relieved to find nothing there. Although they seem to be safe, you are still on your guard as you draw them apart. As you do so, a thunderclap booms outside and makes you jump. But you are safe; a perfectly ordinary window is uncovered.

However, the heavy iron bars on the outside are a little worrying. Through the window you can see nothing but the rain running down the pane of glass. But curiously, the rain is avoiding one area. Could it be that the wind is blowing the rain away from this corner? You bend down to take a closer look. Written in the condensation which has formed on the glass is a *message*! You read three words: 'Mordana in Abaddon'. You repeat this message to yourself and then rub it off the window, in case anyone else should see it. This message may be useful to you (and you will realize when it is). If, later in the adventure, you want to use the message, turn to reference **88**. *Do not turn to* **88** *now!* Now you must head back to the landing and turn left. Turn to **193**.

111

Your host is a little annoyed by your nervousness. 'Come, come,' he says, 'there's no need to be afraid. Has your little accident caused you to lose your nerve? Drink your brandy. You'll soon forget your fears.' As you watch him, your mind begins to play tricks on you. Is his expression one of genuine concern for your welfare, or is there a hint of something secretive in his eyes and smile? You shiver, and your fear of the situation is evident. Add 1 *FEAR* point. A short while later, Franklins appears. 'Your meal is served, sir,' he says to the Earl. You both rise and go through to the dining-room. Turn to **309**.

From behind the door steps a broad-shouldered man with powerful arms

The door opens wide. You are about to step inside but hesitate when you see what lies within. You are entering an underground torture room. In one corner stands a formidable iron maiden, its deadly door standing ajar. A stretching rack is in the centre of the room. Hanging from the ceiling along the left-hand wall are two cages. One is just about large enough for a man to crouch in and the other will allow a man to stand up but not move about. A shiver runs down your spine. Suddenly, two pairs of hands grab your wrists and you are shoved forward into the room! From behind the door steps a broad-shouldered man with powerful arms. He is dressed in a leather apron and trousers and wears a patch across his left eye. 'So!' he exclaims. 'And who do we have here, trespassing in our house? Come on, speak up. Have you lost your tongue?' What will your answer be? Will you tell him you are trying to find your way out and will be happy to leave straight away (turn to **4**) or will you claim to be one of the Master's friends (turn to **16**)?

113

The room you enter is a reception room. A table and six chairs stand in the centre of the room. At one end is an enormous mural of a country scene, perhaps painted of the area, many years ago. On the opposite wall, stretching from the floor to the ceiling, is a full-length mirror. Velvet curtains line the wall opposite the door. You walk over to admire the painting, then turn to face the mirror. A shock is in store. Your eyes widen as you turn towards the mirror and stare into it. *It casts no reflection of you!* Add 1 *FEAR* point. You walk closer to the mirror but still no reflection appears although you can see the table and the wall behind you clearly. You walk right up to it and feel its surface. Your hand passes right through the glass! Pulling it back quickly, you consider the situation. Will you leave this room (turn to **131**), step through the mirror (turn to **160**) or investigate the room further (turn to **324**)?

114

Do you wish to leave the room (turn to **77**) or investigate the box on the mantelpiece (turn to **40**)?

115

Your mouth waters as a roast duck is laid before you. The Earl is having the same, and you both chat as you eat. He wants to know how you came to be driving along this road in the middle of the night, and you tell him about the old man's directions. You ask him about himself and his family. Turn to **28**.

116

Outside the room, the passageway runs onwards, past a door on the left. If you wish to continue along the passageway, turn to **91**. If you wish to explore the area, turn to **166**.

117

You step into the room and close the door behind you. A squeaking noise from one corner makes you jump, but when you walk over you are relieved to find that the squeaking comes from three rats in a cage. You keep your ears peeled for sounds of visitors as you investigate the contents of the room. Do you wish to look through the drawers (turn to **81**), examine the liquids in the glass vials (turn to **341**) or look through the cupboards (turn to **371**)?

118

The door opens and you enter the kitchen. The room is empty and immaculately tidy, with all the knives, pots and pans hanging in neat rows along the walls. A double sink is set under a window, next to a large cooker and fridge. A great square table stands in the centre of the room. There are two doors; one leads outside and the other looks like a pantry door. A large bunch of keys lies on top of the cooker. Do you want:

To try the back door leading outside?   Turn to **327**
To try the other door?   Turn to **126**
To grab the bunch of keys on the cooker?   Turn to **148**

119

Will you start by looking through the ornaments on a corner shelf (turn to **192**) or will you examine the fire and the mantelpiece (turn to **303**)?

120

You grab the door-handle and twist it. The door is locked! The voice laughs at your futile attempt to escape. 'No, my friend,' it chuckles, 'you cannot escape from this room. The only escape you are going to make now is from life itself!' Add 1 *FEAR* point and turn to **291**.

121

You open the door quickly and step out on to the landing. Luckily there is no one about. Turning left, you follow the passage round until you reach a wood-panelled wall where the passage turns left. Turn to **175**.

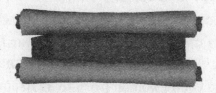

The passageway leads into a large chamber with rocky walls. Mystical symbols are painted on the walls and four goats' heads, mounted on spikes, mark out the central area. In the centre of this area is an altar draped with a black cloth and a hooded figure stands by the altar. This figure wears a gown like the others, but his goat's head is dyed purple. You presume he must be their leader. You follow the congregation, who surround the altar, and stand at the back. A few minutes later, another sound comes from the passage; this time you hear the screams of a young woman. Two of the masked characters emerge from the passageway pulling a pretty fair-haired girl, who is fighting furiously to break free and screaming at the top of her voice. She is dragged to the altar and tied down on it. The congregation, led by their leader, chant for a short time, then the leader motions for Brother Isaacson to step forward. The two exchange masks and Brother Isaacson steps up to the altar. Drawing a sharp dagger from his gown, he raises it above the woman. Excited mutterings run through the crowd. But what will you do? Will you watch what will happen (turn to **314**), will you try to find a way out (turn to **80**) or will you try to rescue the young woman (turn to **328**)?

123

The room you enter looks well lived in. It is a bedroom, and a large bed covered with a yellow bedspread dominates the room. Clothes are strewn about the floor and a tap is running in a wash-basin in the corner. The clothes suggest it is a woman's room, but no one is about. Will you call out to announce yourself in case anyone *is* in the room (turn to **386**), search around to see what you can find (turn to **337**) or leave the room (turn to **2**)?

124

The disembodied head speaks: 'Prepare yourself for death, miserable mortal!' it gloats. 'For the evil that is in this place cannot be escaped. The House of Drumer has drawn you here for one purpose. Before the night is out you will join me and my companions in the nether world. Our fate will be yours. You will forever haunt the place that has caused your death!' With these words, a mocking laughter fills the room. The apparition turns back through the wall and as it does so, the laughter fades. But the fright will give you 2 *FEAR* points. Add these to your total and leave the room. Turn to **382**.

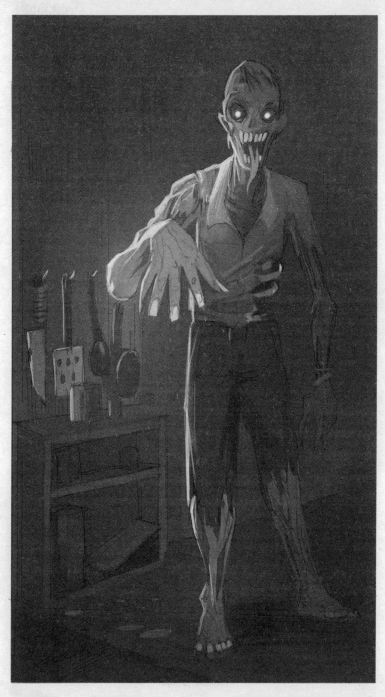

A long tongue flashes out at you and the creature steps forwards

125

You enter a dimly lit bedroom and close the door behind you. The room is empty apart from a dressing-table and a large bed, but you can hear music playing. Do you wish to search the room to make sure it's safe (turn to **239**) or leave straight away and head back to the landing (turn to **272**)?

126

You reach for the door handle and open it wide. But the sight that greets you makes you step back aghast! Inside the pantry, standing motionless, is a hideous figure in tattered clothes. Its face and hands are in a state of semi-decay, and the odour of death fills your nostrils. Your intrusion has woken it. Its eyes open and a hissing noise comes from its throat. A long tongue flashes out at you and the creature steps forward. Add 2 *FEAR* points. You must fight this GHOUL! But you may grab a knife from the wall to use as a WEAPON (add 3 *SKILL* points).

GHOUL   *SKILL 8*   *STAMINA 7*

As soon as it inflicts its second wound on you, turn to **186**. If you manage to defeat it, turn to **29**.

127

'Come on, then,' he says cheerfully. 'Let's go. I'm ready.' You are not sure whether to play along with him or not. You ask him whether he's sure he knows where he's going. 'Oh, that I do, that I do,' he laughs, walking up to you. *'But sure as heaven I'm not going down there without a fight!'* And with those words he pulls a knife from his gown and attacks you. Resolve this battle:

MAN IN WHITE   *SKILL 7*   *STAMINA 9*

If you wish to spare his life, you may turn to **359** when you have reduced his *STAMINA* to 2 points. If you decide to finish him off, turn to **366**.

128

You take a short run and charge at the door. It shudders, and the noise reverberates through the house. But the lock holds firm and you bounce off, clutching a sore arm. Deduct 2 *STAMINA* points for the pain. If you wish to try charging again, turn to **106**. If you feel that the door is too strong and you are unlikely to break it down, turn to **158**.

129

You tiptoe quietly along the wall towards the other passageway. Keeping your eyes on the ceremony to make sure you are not noticed, you edge along until you reach the passage and nip smartly along it. You have escaped! At the end of the passage is a door which is unlocked. You open it. Turn to **232**.

130

Score the points indicated for any of the following choices:

Kelnor	5 points
Kris	3 points

You score no points for any other choice. Now turn to **297**.

131

You leave the room cautiously and look around in the hallway. There is no one in sight. There is a door to your left, which you may try by turning to **211**. Otherwise you may turn right and follow the hallway round (turn to **58**).

132

You walk down the stairs cautiously, looking in every direction. There is no one about. In the hallway below you may choose to try either a door on the left (turn to **353**) or a door on the right (turn to **285**) or you can walk up to the front door and open it (turn to **222**).

133

You step into the small room, which is bare except for a table. Glancing round to make sure you are safe, you walk up to the table. The box which rests on it is a handsome wooden one with brass fastenings. It is long and thin and looks as if it should hold a pair of duelling-pistols. You undo the catch and flip back the lid. Turn to **99**.

134

You bend down and grasp the crate by its corners. With a heave, you lift it into the air. The sight at your feet horrifies you and you must add 2 *FEAR* points for the fright! Out of the upturned box drops the limp body of a lifeless animal! The creature is perhaps a well-shorn sheep or, more likely, a goat, but it is difficult to identify as it has been decapitated. You turn away, fighting down a feeling of nausea and make for the door. Turn to **378**.

135

You place the ring on your finger. As you do so, the man starts to smile. 'Well,' he says, 'that should certainly make my job a good deal easier! Come over here.' You shiver as you realize that you have done the wrong thing! Your fingers desperately try to reach the ring to pull it off, but your mind will not allow them to do so. The ring has brought you directly under the control of your host's will. Turn to **326**.

136

Were you Lucky or Unlucky? If you were Lucky, you managed to escape the splintering glass without harm. If you were Unlucky, the glass cut your wrist – lose 2 *STAMINA* points. Turn now to **317**.

137

You walk up to a large window which looks as though it may not be quite closed. But there are heavy bars across it. Even if you were able to open the window, you would never manage to squeeze through the bars. The house is certainly well protected from intruders! Do you want to continue round the house to see where the light is coming from (turn to **345**) or return to the front door and either pull the rope (turn to **275**) or use the knocker (turn to **357**)?

138

You recognize the Hunchback; he is the man who brought you a drink upstairs, but you cannot be sure he has recognized you. Do you want to stop fighting and jog his memory (turn to **198**) or would you rather just kill him (turn to **164**)?

She is stone-cold! Dead!

139

You step over to the bed and shake the old woman gently. But as soon as you touch her withered skin, you jump back in horror. She is stone-cold! Dead! Add 2 *FEAR* points for the shock. As you stand by the bed, shivering, a low moan comes from the body. Its eyelids flick open and pure white eyes stare up at the ceiling. She has no pupils! Do you wish to wait to see what will happen next (turn to **246**), or will you beat a hasty retreat and return to the passageway (turn to **159**)?

140

You grasp the handle and turn it. The door is locked, and it looks too sturdy for you to break down. Will you turn towards the door at the end of the corridor (turn to **332**) or go back the way you came, carrying on past the room from which you originally appeared (turn to **287**)?

141

Score the points as indicated for any of the following choices:

Shekou	5 points
Shaitan	3 points

You score no points for any other choices. Now turn to **280**.

The footsteps get louder and then they stop. *You cannot see anything!* By the sound of the footsteps, whoever was coming should be standing right in front of you! You start to sweat, and must add 1 *FEAR* point. A pain grips your chest and starts to grow. It is as if an invisible enemy is grasping your heart and squeezing! But you still cannot see anything. You fight the pain and resounding laughter echoes in your ears. Something *is* standing there! You struggle to escape. Fight this INVISIBLE ENEMY. Although you will do him no harm, his *STAMINA* score reflects the grip which he has on you; if you reduce his *STAMINA* to zero, you will break free and can escape by running down the hallway and turning right. Turn to **257** if you escape:

INVISIBLE ENEMY   *SKILL 10*   *STAMINA 4*

143

You step over to the next cell. The sound of footsteps outside the door makes you turn quickly. Four men dressed in white gowns and wearing goats' heads appear at the door. 'I told you!' says one. I knew I could hear something. Looks like someone wants to free our prisoners. Come on, brothers!' They rush towards you and you must resolve your battle with their leader, who attacks you first:

LEADER   *SKILL 8*   *STAMINA 9*

If you win, turn to **301**.

144

'Who's that?' asks a voice from behind the door. The door is unlocked, so you could walk in, but perhaps you don't want to be discovered just yet. Will you open the door and take a chance with whoever is in the room (turn to **71**) or will you mumble something like, 'Sorry, wrong door,' then try elsewhere (turn to **278**)?

145

How will you hold off these advancing creatures? Will you pick up the brandy decanter (turn to **169**) or move slowly backwards towards the window (turn to **64**)?

146

The rock creaks and dust rises as the wall starts to move. A crack appears in the brickwork and slowly a secret door opens. But to your surprise, the door opens on to one side of the hollow area you found. Perhaps this was merely a decoy. Moments later the door has opened wide enough to let you see inside. You can see a small chamber with a table standing in the centre. On the table is a box. If you wish to enter, turn to **133**. If you would rather leave, you can climb the stairs and go through the door at the top (turn to **293**).

147

Where will you hide? Will you nip behind the curtains (turn to **184**) or quickly dive through the mirror (turn to **3**)?

148

You pick up the bunch of keys and start to flick through them. *Aaaarrgghhh!* You scream loudly and drop the keys on the floor. For they are red hot, and you have severely burnt your hand! You were using your weapon-hand, and must lose 3 *STAMINA* and 2 *SKILL* points; but if you wish, you may *Test your Luck*. A Lucky roll means that you weren't using your weapon-hand after all, and you only lose 1 *STAMINA* point. The scream and clatter of the falling keys have made quite a noise. Turn to **254**.

149

You take the stopper off the vial and sniff the liquid. It is odourless. Raising the neck to your lips, you take a sip and wait for something to happen – but nothing does. You feel no strange effects at all. Turn to **385**.

150

As you are puzzling over the curtains, you reach out to lean on the bed. But as you rest your weight on the bedpost, the whole bed shifts aside and you crash down on to the floor! This is all very strange – and a little scary. Add 1 *FEAR* point and take 1 *STAMINA* point of damage. A rumbling from the opposite side of the room breaks into your thoughts. Sliding over the carpet towards you, and accelerating rapidly, is one of the chairs. *Test your Luck*. If you are Lucky, turn to **101**. If you are Unlucky, turn to **53**.

151

A plaque beneath the painting reads 'Lady Margaret of Danvers: 1802–1834'. You stand and admire her beauty and wonder why she died so young. As you are staring at her face, you suddenly blink and look again. Didn't you just see her *lips moving!* Surely not! A whisper reaches your ears but you cannot make out its message. You lean forwards and put your ear to the lips. A soft woman's voice is speaking to you: 'Stranger, beware of this place, for it is cursed! Many have succumbed to its power, myself included. The evil Lord Kelnor will already be plotting your death. Drink not his white wine. Or if you can, begone. Escape while you may!' You step back, aghast! What sort of place is this? A creepy, rundown old building filled with priceless antiques – and paintings which *talk?* A cold prickle runs down your neck and you must add 1 *FEAR* point. Will you now run for the door (turn to **391**) or wait to see what happens (turn to **277**)?

152

You try the door-handle. It will not turn; the door is locked! A rush of anxiety comes over you. How will you leave this room? Add 1 *FEAR* point. Again you try the doorknob, but it will not budge. A noise comes from behind you and you swing round. Did that rustling sound come from the window? You step over to investigate. Turn to **236**.

153

'Is that so?' he asks. 'Then why are you here?' Will you tell him that you are an outsider trying to escape from the house (turn to **208**) or will you pretend to be a servant of the Earl of Drumer (turn to **268**)?

154

You try the door of the Asmodeus room. It is locked, but the key is in the lock. You turn it and step into a dimly lit room. A single candle is burning on a table on the far side of the room, in front of a window. Two packing crates have been turned upside down to make seats on either side of the table and there is no other furniture. Your ears prick up at a shuffling sound behind you and you wheel round towards the door. A loud cry comes from behind the door and a man with thick white hair launches himself at you! He is dressed in a long robe of a dirty grey colour and before you can avoid him, he is on top of you! Add 1 *FEAR* point. Resolve your battle with him:

WHITE-HAIRED MAN   *SKILL 7*   *STAMINA 9*

When you have inflicted your first wound on him, turn to **162**.

155

You step into the room. It is a stylish bedchamber, beautifully decorated. But one thing disturbs you immediately. *The windows are barred.* Perhaps, being so far from anywhere, they are designed to keep intruders out, rather than to keep guests in! In the centre of the room is a four-poster bed. You walk over and test the mattress; it feels very comfortable. By now you are in need of a rest. Will you climb into bed (turn to **231**) or walk over to the window to take a look outside (turn to **27**)?

156

You take a book off the shelf entitled: *Mystical Symbols and Their Part in Magic Rituals*. You open the cover and something drops out of the book on to the floor. You bend down to pick it up. It is a pentacle, fashioned in metal and hanging on a long chain. The book itself is hollowed out to take the charm and a piece of paper lies underneath it. The paper describes the pentacle as having powers over devil-worshippers. Cast into the pentacle is the number 66. If you wish to take the pentacle, you may use it at any appropriate time by turning to reference number **66**. Add 2 *LUCK* points for your find. Do you now wish to look for other interesting books (turn to **286**) or would you prefer to leave the room (turn to **54**)?

157

'Hmmm,' grunts the torturer, 'I am still not convinced. Nevertheless, you *may* be a friend of the Master.' You hold your breath as he pauses to make up his mind. 'All right, stranger, I will give you the benefit of the doubt. Release the rack, Dirk.' You are set free and allowed to leave the room. Turn to **248**.

158

You can hear slow footsteps approaching your room. They stop outside the room and a key rattles as it unlocks your door! You must quickly decide whether to jump into bed and pretend to be asleep (turn to **179**) or to hide behind the door to surprise whoever is about to come in (turn to **373**).

159

Having explored most of the rooms upstairs, you decide to risk searching the ground floor. You follow the landing back round to the staircase and creep downstairs. Turn to **132**.

160

Behind the mirror is a small chamber, just large enough for you to turn around in. There are two doors in the chamber. Do you want to try the left-hand door (turn to **92**) or the right-hand door (turn to **294**)? Or would you rather step back through the mirror (turn to **349**)?

161

You unstopper the vial and sniff the liquid. It smells of lemon. You raise the neck to your lips and take a sip. It *tastes* like lemon juice! You swallow it down and wait anxiously for any effects. Nothing happens. But this is understandable, as the effects of this liquid will not become apparent until you have your next fight. For the liquid has healing powers and will protect you from injury. The sip you took was strong enough to heal the next two wounds you take; do not deduct any *STAMINA* points for these wounds. Now turn to **385**.

162

Your attacker reels from the blow and you have a moment to catch your breath and consider what to do next. Will you:

Leap in and finish him off?	Turn to **271**
Hold up your hands to indicate you mean no harm?	Turn to **313**
Run for the door opposite?	Turn to **378**

163

On the bedside table are a candle, which lights the room, and a silver tray. On the silver tray is a night-time snack: bread, jam and tea. You can, if you wish, eat this snack (turn to **226**). Otherwise you can leave it and either investigate the cupboards (turn to **43**) or leave the room (turn to **243**).

164

You knock him to the ground and are able to get a vicious kick in before the Hunchback can recover. Deduct an extra 2 *STAMINA* points from him and resolve the battle. If you win, turn to **116**.

165

You search around the corner but can find nothing unusual. You can hear some bats squeaking and the overwhelming smell of their droppings forces you to cut short your search. You must decide what you want to do next. Will you search under the stairs (turn to **61**), look along the back wall (turn to **356**) or climb the stairs (turn to **293**)?

166

Exploring the area, you find nothing particularly unusual. You see a wooden door on the left of the passageway, which you may try by turning to **221**, or you can walk a little further up and try another door in the right-hand wall (turn to **209**). If you would prefer to ignore the doors and continue up the passageway, turn to **91**.

167

The sheets do, in fact, cover up furniture and boxes. There are several easy chairs and a stylish chaise-longue, and the boxes contain household bits and pieces. One box contains ornamental crockery wrapped up in newspaper. There is nothing unusual about any of this. Turn to **380**.

The figure is almost human, but its head is missing

168

A soft voice is calling your name! You leap back against a wall, while across the room a strange shape is forming. A human figure is passing through the very wall itself and entering the room. At least, the figure is *almost* human, but its head is missing. As it materializes before you, the voice becomes clearer. It comes from a head that is carried, not on the apparition's shoulders, but in its hand which hangs down at its side! The sight is horrible and ghostly blood drips on to the carpet from the severed head. You must add 2 *FEAR* points. Will you stay to hear what the ghost has to say to you (turn to **124**), or run from the room (turn to **382**)?

169

You grab the decanter and splash brandy quickly over the two creatures, hoping to douse their flames. But to your dismay, the brandy burns fiercely! In fact it seems to nourish the Fire Sprites rather than weaken them. Turn to **9**.

170

'What business of yours is this house?' she screams. 'If you will not go of your own accord, then my hounds will see you off. And if they cannot, I will do it myself!' With these words, a wooden panel slides open in the wall. Two huge GREAT DANES spring out and attack. Resolve your battle with the dogs (fight them one at a time):

	SKILL	STAMINA
First GREAT DANE	7	6
Second GREAT DANE	6	6

If you defeat the dogs, you may either leave the room (turn to **159**) or remain to search it (turn to **19**).

171

Your struggles are wasted. You cannot free yourself from the sheets and the pillow, which are wrapping themselves around your body and face. Eventually, you drop back into the bed. You have fallen victim to the evil within the House of Drumer.

172

Caution should have overruled your appetite. For in the House of Drumer, cheese and white wine are not recommended, for the simple reason that anyone who eats cheese or drinks white wine will pay the penalty. They are poisoned! This is the end of your adventure.

173

You open your eyes. Your head is spinning and it is some time before you are fully aware of the fact that your hands and feet are bound. The room you are in is empty, but you work out a plan. You will hop over to the window, break the glass, and use it to cut yourself free. Pulling yourself to your feet is awkward, but you manage it and with a mixture of hops and shuffles you arrive at the window. Outside the wind is blowing the rain against the window panes. Will you go ahead and smash the window with your hands – something of a risky business – or will you instead *Test your Luck?* If you want to *Test your Luck,* turn to **136**. If you do not wish to use your *LUCK* here, turn to **360**.

174

The rock creaks and dust rises as the wall comes to life. A crack appears in the brickwork and slowly a secret door opens. But to your surprise, the door opens to one side of the hollow area you found. Perhaps this was merely a decoy. Moments later the door has opened wide enough to let you see inside. You can see a small chamber with a table standing in the centre. On the table is a box. If you wish to enter, turn to **48**. If you would rather leave, you can climb the stairs and go through the door at the top (turn to **293**).

175

You follow the passageway round the corner to the left. Two doors face each other across the passage and you may either try the door on the left, to the Belial room, or the door on the right, to the Abaddon room. Straight ahead, the passageway continues for a few metres before ending at an unmarked door. Will you:

Try the door of the Belial room?	Turn to **312**
Try the door of the Abaddon room?	Turn to **335**
Try the unmarked door ahead?	Turn to **103**
Turn back and go downstairs?	Turn to **132**

176

'Enough!' shouts the torturer. 'Undo the imposter's ropes. Our friend is no more a friend of the Master than is the Chief of Police!' You are bound to admit he is right, and you try to excuse yourself by saying that you thought you must try that story, otherwise you would have been killed. You tell him the real story of your arrival. Turn to **4**.

177

He frowns and considers your story. 'It is impossible,' he says, 'that your story is true. But somehow you are not like the others. Perhaps there is some truth in what you say – and I would dearly like to find a friend in this evil house. All right, stranger, I believe you.' You breathe a sigh of relief and you can now ask him either how you can escape from the house (turn to **75**) or how you can defeat the Master (turn to **105**)?

178

You immediately turn to aid your comrade, but you are too late. A thrust from the Devil-Worshipper's knife pierces his chest. You slam your fist into the back of the man's neck and he slumps to the floor. But you have lost your ally and must leave without him. Turn to **366**.

179

You spring into the bed and wrap the sheets around you, keeping one eye open just wide enough to see what is going on. A shambling figure enters the room. It looks like a man who is bent over double and he is carrying a glass of liquid in his hand. Placing the glass on your bedside table, he turns to leave the room. Do you want to leap out of bed and attack him (turn to **399**) or will you wait until he has gone and swallow the drink he has left for you (turn to **45**)?

180

The sight before you is the last you will ever see. The wound you have just suffered and the butler's terrifying transformation are more than you can bear. Franklins is no more. His human shell has dissolved and he now stands before you as his true self – a hideous demonic form surrounded by a cloud of vapour. Steam hisses from its mouth and blood – your own blood – drips, not from a knife, but from a huge savage claw that is its right hand. As you drop dying to the floor, this creature from hell steps forwards to crush you with its goat-like hooves. You may have defeated the Earl of Drumer, but not THE MASTER...

A transformation is taking place!

181

The butler screams as your blow strikes him. The man is obviously not the violent type, as the agony in his voice is certainly not warranted by your modest hit. His cry continues! It becomes deafening and you are forced to step back and cover your ears with your hands. But this is not the anguish of an injured man...

Steam begins to rise from the floor and it engulfs the butler. His expression changes from a scream to a vicious snarl and his eyes widen. A transformation is taking place! Before your eyes, the form of Franklins melts away and is replaced by a hideous demonic beast! Steam hisses from its mouth. Its scaly skin is dark. Its hands are now two vicious claws which slash the air before you. Its feet have become hooves – goat-like hooves. You must add 3 *FEAR* points as you witness the creation of this demon from the depths of hell. If you are still alive, turn to **109** if you are using the Kris knife, or **52** if you are not.

182

The man looks away as you pull out your knife and prepare
to strike him with it. 'Again, my thanks,' he says. 'I will not
get another chance to thank you.' Your hand comes down
and even you must close your eyes as you strike him. But
your knife never reaches its target. A strong hand catches
your wrist inches from the man's chest and squeezes
hard. You open your eyes and see the man smiling at
you devilishly. He has tricked you! He had no wish to end
his life. He simply wanted a weapon to use against his
jailers, a weapon which you have now provided for him!
He slams your wrist against the bars, forcing you to drop
the knife inside his cell. Your anger turns to fear when he
does not release his grip, but instead bends down to pick
up the knife and holds it against your throat. 'I am sorry,
my friend,' he says, 'but I cannot risk your telling the
others that I am now armed. My friends and I *must* have
our freedom at any cost. We shall have it when our jailer
returns with our next meal. I am deeply sorry that the
price of our freedom is so high – for you.' And with those
words his blade bites deep. Your adventure ends here.

183

The door opens slowly. A small, stocky man steps into
the room. He appears to be bent double and as he peers
into the room, you leap on him to attack. Turn to **56** to

resolve the battle, but since you leapt on him straight away, you may cause him 2 *STAMINA* points of damage immediately for your surprise attack.

184

You hide behind the curtains, clutching your box, and wait for your visitors to leave. The door opens and you can hear two voices talking. They are discussing a ceremony which involves goats and priests. You hear a click and a moment later, the voices start shouting. They have discovered that the box is missing! You hear angry footsteps stomping about the room and your mouth dries as you wait anxiously to see whether you will be discovered. Suddenly the curtains are flung apart! Sheepishly you stand there holding your box while two men, wild-haired and furious, glare at you. Will you apologize and offer them their box back (turn to **17**) or leap forward and attack them (turn to **215**)?

185

There are no signs of traps in the room. If you wish to double-check, you may *Test your Luck*. If you are Lucky, turn to **379**. If you are Unlucky, turn to **206**. If you do not wish to *Test your Luck,* pull the rope and turn to **318**.

186

This Ghoul has the ability to paralyse you if it is able to inflict four wounds during one fight. You are half-way there and you must be very careful as you continue the battle; two more wounds and you will die. Now return to **126** and finish the fight.

187

As you creep along the wall, someone in the group cries out. You have been spotted. All eyes turn towards you and the unholy gathering advances to surround you. You are trapped. Will you attempt to fight your way out (turn to **365**), or do you have something else you can use? If so, use it.

188

The rock creaks and dust rises as the wall comes to life. A crack appears in the brickwork and slowly a secret door opens. But to your surprise, the door opens on to one side of the hollow area you found. Perhaps this was merely a decoy. Moments later the door has opened wide enough to let you see inside. You can see a small chamber with a table standing in the centre. On the table is a box. If you wish to enter, turn to **133**. If you would rather leave, you can climb the stairs and go through the door at the top (turn to **293**).

189

The Vampire's eyes light up as you open the door. Although you didn't know it, this was just what he was hoping for! As the light from the room falls on to the faces of the Vampire's two undead slaves, their eyes open and they step out of the cupboard towards you. The hideous, grey-green, decaying faces of two ZOMBIES follow you as you step away from them. 'Attack! Attack!' yells the Vampire. They obey. Resolve your combat with them, one at a time:

	SKILL	STAMINA
First ZOMBIE	7	6
Second ZOMBIE	6	6

If you defeat the Zombies, turn to **20**.

190

You knock loudly and watch the window. A few seconds later, the two men reappear and light the candles. The older man walks towards the door. Turn to **207**.

191

As you pull out your weapon, he steps backwards in fear. You demand that he tells you the secrets of the cellars. 'All right, all right,' he pleads, 'I'll tell you. But I will be in terrible trouble if the Master finds out that I am giving away his secrets.' You tell him that he will be in even worse trouble if he *doesn't* tell you what you want to know. 'The cellar rooms,' he starts, 'are connected by secret doors. Some of these are simply hidden, but a few – the most important ones – need a password to open them. The Master keeps on changing the password to keep his secrets safe.' You ask him what the current password is, but he says he doesn't know. You threaten him again, and he starts to fight:

HUNCHBACK　　　　*SKILL 7*　　　　*STAMINA 7*

When you have inflicted your first wound on him, turn to **284**.

192

There are several delicate items of pottery and a few silver pieces on the shelf. One of the silver ornaments is a short dagger, and you may take this with you if you want. It is rather too short to be a really useful

WEAPON, but nevertheless, you may add 2 *SKILL* points if you use it in a fight. There is also a silver hip-flask. If you have not already done so, you may take this flask and fill it with brandy. Now you may either examine the fireplace (turn to **303**) or leave the room (turn to **218**).

193

A short distance further on, you come to the top of the main staircase which leads downwards. Immediately opposite the staircase is an unmarked door. Do you wish to go downstairs (turn to **132**), try the unmarked door (turn to **377**), or will you continue round the landing (turn to **233**)?

194

Score the points as indicated if you wrote down any of the following words:

Azazel	3 points
Abaddon	5 points
Asmodeus	3 points
Apollyon	3 points

You score no points for any other choice. Now turn to **130**.

Slowly the complete message forms

195

The room is a study. Old leather-bound books line the walls and the only source of light comes from a single candle burning on an antique desk. You walk over to examine the desk, which is made from beautiful wood and has brass-handled drawers. A piece of paper rests on the blotter. As you look at it, you are suddenly aware that something strange is happening. A large brown letter F is forming in the top left-hand corner! You gasp as the word 'Find' appears in a child's handwriting across the top of the paper. For this you must add 1 *FEAR* point. Slowly the complete message forms: 'Find Shekou.' Who or what is Shekou? You pick up the paper and move round the desk to see it more clearly in the light. But as quickly as it appeared, the message disappears. Do you wish to look over the collection of books (turn to **62**) or will you leave this room (turn to **54**)?

196

A rack of lamb is brought in on a silver platter. The smell is delicious! You both start to eat and talk. The Earl asks you about your job and your reason for being in such an out-of-the-way place in the middle of the night. In turn, he tells you about himself and his family. Turn to **28**.

197

You walk up to the mantelpiece and pick up the box. A catch is holding it shut. But before you open the box, a rustling from the window attracts your attention. *Something is happening!* You place the box back on the mantelpiece and walk over to the curtains. Turn to **236**.

198

The dull-witted Hunchback seems to vaguely remember your face. You start to chat to him and find that he is quite flattered that *someone* wants to talk to him. He tells you his name is Shekou and he lives in the cellars beneath the house. Do you wish to ask him about the secrets of his cellars (turn to **18**) or, if you have any brandy with you, you may pull it out and offer him a drink (turn to **93**).

199

You sit on your haunches and reach for the photograph. As you pick it up, you feel a heavy *thud* on the top of your head! You slump to the floor, dazed, and the plant-pot, which came crashing down on your head, smashes on the floor. You must lose 3 *STAMINA* points for this accident. Now turn to **290**.

200

You open the door and peer round. The room is a large, elegantly decorated bedroom, with a four-poster bed in one corner. There is a three-piece suite in the centre of the room, facing a fireplace. A fire is smouldering, but the room appears to be empty. On the far side of the room are two more doors. Do you wish to go in (turn to **69**) or quickly close the door and leave the room (turn to **389**)?

201

You are bundled inside the small cage and hoisted into the air. What a dreadful place to spend your days. The cage is big enough for you to sit inside, with your knees close up to your chest. But you are unable to stretch at all. When cramp sets in, your fate will be long, slow and painful, much to the delight of the torturer and his assistants...

202

You tell the man you have no wish to team up with him. The door is unlocked and he is free to go whenever he pleases. Now where will you go? Turn to **278**.

203

There is only one hiding-place in the room, but you will have to be lucky to find it. *Test your Luck*. If you are Lucky, turn to **376**. If you are Unlucky, you will have to wait to see who – or what – your visitor is. But you may decide to wait behind the door, instead of in plain view (turn to **369**).

204

Do you wish to try the other door (turn to **92**) or would you prefer to step back through the mirror (turn to **349**)?

205

The door is firmly locked. Try the door opposite by turning to **118**.

206

You can find no signs of any traps. Ring for the butler by turning to **318**.

207

'What's this?' you hear the older man ask. 'Someone knocking at the door at this time of night? Could it be one of the brethren? I thought everyone was here.' Then the two men start whispering to each other in voices too low for you to hear. You wait patiently outside in the rain until eventually, the door opens and a voice asks, 'Who is it?' Will you tell them about your predicament and ask to use the phone (turn to **95**) or will you claim to be one of the brethren that you heard them talking about (turn to **267**)?

208

'I don't believe it!' he exclaims. 'Have my prayers been answered? Can I join you? Please, you must allow me to come with you. I can be of great help to you.' You tell him he is certainly welcome to help in your escape, and ask him how he came to be in this hidden area. 'Do you know about the sacrifices?' he asks. 'Well, I am to be saved for the next ceremony. I was part of the Master's coven but my conscience will no longer allow me to live with the evil it entails. But the coven cannot allow defectors. I was sentenced to death – death by sacrifice! Together we must destroy Kelnor, the Master. I know how it can be done! Kelnor can only be killed with the Kris dagger which is hidden somewhere in the house. And he must be summoned in a *red room*. Let us agree to rid the world of this human monster and his evil sect!' You would be foolish to refuse the help and agree. You may add 1 *LUCK* point for this information. A noise outside cuts the conversation short – someone is coming! Turn to **87**.

209

This room seems to be a dungeon of some sort, for along one wall are four cells with heavy iron bars locking their occupants in. No one seems to be on *your* side of the bars, so you walk in to have a look. A twig cracks as you step forward and immediately three bodies spring to life in three of the cells. They are a ragged lot – clothes in tatters, hair dishevelled and grubby. They all reach forward through the bars and plead with you to release them. Each one has been captured by the Earl of Drumer's servants and imprisoned to await some horrendous fate. Nearest to you is a pretty young girl; her face and fair hair are dirty and she is in tears. She desperately wants to be released. In the second cell is a tall man with strong features. He has accepted that he is about to die and bravely asks you to kill him now, to deprive the evil Earl of his pleasure. In the third cell is a balding man in a grey gown who says nothing. Do you wish to try to help these prisoners? You may talk to one of them if you wish. Would you like to talk to the young girl (turn to **322**), the dark man (turn to **266**) or the balding man (turn to **363**). If you would rather not talk to any of them, you may leave the room and walk away (turn to **91**).

210

As you leave the room, the Hunchback limps along,

muttering to himself, 'I wish the Master's friends would not just drop in on me like that,' he mumbles, 'giving me such a fright and all. Especially on a night like tonight...' He leads you along until he reaches a door on the left. 'Keep on going until you reach a staircase, then go up into the house. I've got work to do down here.' Do you recognize this Hunchback? Have you met him before? If so, you may turn to **230**. If not, you may either follow his directions (turn to **393**) or wait until he has gone and explore the cellar (turn to **166**).

211

The door is locked and you will not be able to open it. You turn round and follow the hallway (turn to **58**).

212

Your key does not fit in the lock. The door remains firmly closed. Turn to **47**.

213

The table is quite ordinary. You feel around underneath it, but can find nothing exceptional there. The packing crate on the left feels light. You tip it up to have a look underneath and find nothing inside. But the crate on the right is heavy. You kick it with your foot and it does not move. Do you want to lift it to see what is hidden inside (turn to **134**) or leave it alone and walk back out into the hallway (turn to **378**)?

214

You tell him who you are and that you wish to escape from the house too, preferably destroying the Earl of Drumer's cult of terror on the way. The man begins to get quite excited. 'My name is Rafferty,' he says. 'I have seen enough of the evil in this place and wish to wash it out of my life for ever. Perhaps we can escape together. There is a secret trap-door in the ceiling in this corner of the room. If you will be so kind as to bend over, I will climb on your back; and when I'm through I can haul you up.' Will you help him with his plan to escape (turn to **245**) or do you suspect this character and decide you would rather continue alone (turn to **202**)?

215

The two men are as startled as you are by this encounter, but you are ready to attack. You drop the leather box and leap forward. Resolve this battle (fight the men one at a time):

	SKILL	STAMINA
First MAN	7	8
Second MAN	8	9

If you wish to *Escape* at any time during the battle after the first four Attack Rounds, you may only do so by throwing yourself through the mirror while they are not looking (turn to **160**). If you defeat the two men, turn to **273**.

216

The narrow stairway splits and offers you two ways down. Will you choose the left-hand stairs (turn to **398**) or the right-hand stairs (turn to **89**)?

217

The door opens at the top of a staircase which leads down into the cellars underneath the house. You walk downstairs slowly to allow your eyes to become accustomed to the darkness. At the foot of the stairs, a twittering noise catches your attention. Suddenly you feel something land on your head and dig sharp claws into your scalp! You swat it away and, your hand touches a small, leathery body. BATS! A number of them are flapping around your head, darting and scratching with their claws. You must add 1 *FEAR* point for the shock, and you may now:

Run back upstairs	Turn to **370**
Hide under the stairs	Turn to **320**
Fight the bats	Turn to **343**

218

Did you enter this drawing-room from the hallway or the study? If you entered from the hallway, you take the door which leads into the study – turn to **195**. If you entered from the study, you go through the other door into the hallway. Turn to **251**.

219

As the others set off along the passageway, you remain

215

The two men are as startled as you are by this encounter, but you are ready to attack. You drop the leather box and leap forward. Resolve this battle (fight the men one at a time):

	SKILL	STAMINA
First MAN	7	8
Second MAN	8	9

If you wish to *Escape* at any time during the battle after the first four Attack Rounds, you may only do so by throwing yourself through the mirror while they are not looking (turn to **160**). If you defeat the two men, turn to **273**.

216

The narrow stairway splits and offers you two ways down. Will you choose the left-hand stairs (turn to **398**) or the right-hand stairs (turn to **89**)?

217

The door opens at the top of a staircase which leads down into the cellars underneath the house. You walk downstairs slowly to allow your eyes to become accustomed to the darkness. At the foot of the stairs, a twittering noise catches your attention. Suddenly you feel something land on your head and dig sharp claws into your scalp! You swat it away and, your hand touches a small, leathery body. BATS! A number of them are flapping around your head, darting and scratching with their claws. You must add 1 *FEAR* point for the shock, and you may now:

Run back upstairs	Turn to **370**
Hide under the stairs	Turn to **320**
Fight the bats	Turn to **343**

218

Did you enter this drawing-room from the hallway or the study? If you entered from the hallway, you take the door which leads into the study – turn to **195**. If you entered from the study, you go through the other door into the hallway. Turn to **251**.

219

As the others set off along the passageway, you remain

at the back of the crowd. As the last few are leaving the room, another man bursts in through the door, puffing and panting. 'Good, I'm not too late,' he gasps. 'For a minute I thought I'd miss it! Now let's see. Where is my gown and mask?' Your blood chills as the man starts looking in the area where you took your costume. 'Gone!' he says. 'Wait, Brothers, someone has taken my dress. Ah, *there* is my mask. Sorry, Brother, you must have taken mine by mistake. I can recognize it quite clearly by the broken tooth. Here, let me have it.' The man snatches the mask from your head and all attention is focused on you. 'Here, who are you?' someone asks. Your hesitant reply gives the game away. 'Back, Brothers!' shouts a voice. 'We seem to have an intruder in our midst.' A dozen men come back into the room and surround you. You have no choice but to go with them to the cell where they lock you in. This is a cell from which there is no escape; your adventure is over.

220

The poor, miserable creature pleads for mercy. He is such a pitiful sight that you step back as he grovels on the floor. He will do you no harm and thanks you continually for sparing his life. Do you now wish to leave the room, locking him in behind you (turn to **350**) or will you try to force him to answer your questions (turn to **234**)?

Standing in the doorway before you is a hooded figure!

221

You can hear gruff noises coming from within the room. Whoever, or whatever, is in there certainly doesn't sound too friendly. Will you try the door anyway (turn to **344**) or will you open the door in the wall opposite (turn to **209**) or continue along the passageway (turn to **91**)?

222

You grip the handle, turn it and slowly pull the door open. The noise of the storm raging outside becomes louder. You start to walk through the doorway, but stop and gasp, your eyes frozen wide open! Standing in the doorway before you is a hooded figure! But its face is not human. Instead, the head is that of a goat and its mouth is red with blood, which is dripping on to the ground. Its dead eyes stare vacantly upwards. The sight is terrifying and you must add 3 *FEAR* points. You slam the door in its face and turn around. Where will you run – through a door on the right (turn to **353**), through a door on the left (turn to **285**) or back down the hallway (turn to **108**)?

223

The rock creaks and dust rises as the wall starts to move. A crack appears down the wall in the brickwork and slowly a secret door opens. But to your surprise, the door opens on to one side of the hollow area you found. Perhaps this was merely a decoy. Moments later, the door has opened wide enough to let you see inside. You can see a small chamber with a table standing in the centre. On the table is a box. If you wish to enter, turn to **133**. If you would rather leave, you can climb the stairs and go through the door at the top (turn to **293**).

224

Franklins brings them to you and you finish off your meal. 'Well, my friend,' says the Earl, 'you must now be quite tired; it is well past midnight. Franklins will show you to your room.' You thank him and follow the butler out of the dining-room. 'This way, if you please,' he says as he leads you up a magnificent wide staircase with carved wooden banisters. A landing at the top leads to various different rooms, each with a name-plaque on the door. He takes you to one which reads 'Erasmus Room' and opens the door, wishing you a good night's sleep. Turn to **5**.

221

You can hear gruff noises coming from within the room. Whoever, or whatever, is in there certainly doesn't sound too friendly. Will you try the door anyway (turn to **344**) or will you open the door in the wall opposite (turn to **209**) or continue along the passageway (turn to **91**)?

222

You grip the handle, turn it and slowly pull the door open. The noise of the storm raging outside becomes louder. You start to walk through the doorway, but stop and gasp, your eyes frozen wide open! Standing in the doorway before you is a hooded figure! But its face is not human. Instead, the head is that of a goat and its mouth is red with blood, which is dripping on to the ground. Its dead eyes stare vacantly upwards. The sight is terrifying and you must add 3 *FEAR* points. You slam the door in its face and turn around. Where will you run – through a door on the right (turn to **353**), through a door on the left (turn to **285**) or back down the hallway (turn to **108**)?

223

The rock creaks and dust rises as the wall starts to move. A crack appears down the wall in the brickwork and slowly a secret door opens. But to your surprise, the door opens on to one side of the hollow area you found. Perhaps this was merely a decoy. Moments later, the door has opened wide enough to let you see inside. You can see a small chamber with a table standing in the centre. On the table is a box. If you wish to enter, turn to **133**. If you would rather leave, you can climb the stairs and go through the door at the top (turn to **293**).

224

Franklins brings them to you and you finish off your meal. 'Well, my friend,' says the Earl, 'you must now be quite tired; it is well past midnight. Franklins will show you to your room.' You thank him and follow the butler out of the dining-room. 'This way, if you please,' he says as he leads you up a magnificent wide staircase with carved wooden banisters. A landing at the top leads to various different rooms, each with a name-plaque on the door. He takes you to one which reads 'Erasmus Room' and opens the door, wishing you a good night's sleep. Turn to **5**.

225

You press the button. It clicks and you can hear a rumbling from behind the bookcase. Slowly, the bookcase slides aside to reveal a passageway behind it. If you wish to go down the passage, turn to **241**. If you would rather not risk exploring the passage, leave the study by turning to **54**.

226

You examine the tray carefully, but there seems to be nothing suspicious about it. The snack is just what you needed! You may add 4 *STAMINA* points and 1 *LUCK* point for this find. When you are ready, you may either leave the room (turn to **243**) or investigate the cupboards (turn to **43**).

227

What food did you take? Bread and cakes will restore 2 *STAMINA* points each; dried meats, dried fish and cheese will restore 1 *STAMINA* point each; fruit and wine will not restore any. Wine will lose you 1 *SKILL* point, but if you drank wine you may deduct 2 *FEAR* points (Dutch courage!). If you ate cheese or drank white wine, turn to **172**. If you ate neither of these, but ate dried fish or drank red wine, turn to **84**. If you ate none of these, turn to **36**.

228

How will you attack the man? Will you use a weapon (turn to **32**) or do you have anything else you can use (turn to **46**)?

229

You follow the landing round until you reach another door on the right-hand side. A name-plate identifies it as the Erasmus room. If you wish to enter this room, turn to **140**. Ahead of you, at the end of the passageway, is another door. If you wish to go there, turn to **332**.

230

You recognize the Hunchback as the man who brought you a drink upstairs. Will you jog his memory (turn to **198**) or would you rather have your revenge and attack him (turn to **302**)?

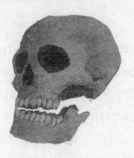

231

You climb into bed and blow out the candle. Anxious thoughts race through your mind. The old man who gave you wrong directions, your accident, the sinister atmosphere in the house... Soon your weariness gets the better of you and you drift off to sleep. In a disturbed slumber you begin to dream. You are being chased by a swirling cloud of gas. You are trying to run from it but the faster you run, the slower you go. The cloud is catching you. As you desperately try to avoid it, it engulfs you. You begin to cough and choke. It is stifling your breath! You wake with a start. Your head is buried in the pillow and the bedclothes are holding you down! They feel heavy and you must strain to fight for air. Add 2 *FEAR* points as you realize that something supernatural is happening here. To determine whether or not you escape from the pillow, roll two dice. If the total is less than or equal to your *SKILL* score, turn to **348**. If it is higher than your *SKILL* score turn to **171**.

232

The door opens into a small room which is pitch-black. There seems to be no exit from the room, but you feel around the walls. Eventually your hand touches a small button in one corner and you press this. A panel in front of you slides aside and lets you out into a passageway. There are two doors opposite each other, one on the left and one on the right. There is no other way through. Will you try the door on the left (turn to **342**) or the door on the right (turn to **144**)?

233

A few steps past the unmarked door is *another* unmarked door. If you wish to try this one, turn to **98**. If you wish to ignore it and go on, turn to **374**.

234

He is terrified of you and agrees to answer your questions in exchange for his miserable life. Do you wish to ask him:

How you can escape from the house?	Turn to **258**
About the people in the house?	Turn to **308**
What is happening in the house?	Turn to **325**

235

If you wrote down any of the following words, you can score the points indicated:

Diabolus	3 points
Drumer	5 points

Any other choice is not worth any points. Turn to **194**.

Its wide eyes stare at you, yet through you

236

From behind the curtain, a heavy blow hits you in the chest and knocks you backwards on to the floor. Lose 2 *STAMINA* points and add 2 *FEAR* points. You pick yourself up quickly and the curtain slides to one side. A human figure steps out. Its skin is a dirty-green colour. Its wide eyes stare *at* you, yet *through* you. Its jaw gapes open to reveal a mouth half full of rotten teeth. It wears ragged clothes. And it is advancing towards you! Resolve your fight with this ZOMBIE:

ZOMBIE   *SKILL 7*   *STAMINA 6*

If you defeat the Zombie, turn to **114**.

237

You stand back from the secret door and say your password. Which word will you choose?

Pravemi	Turn to **223**
Goathead	Turn to **188**
Murder	Turn to **174**
Kris	Turn to **146**

238

There is no telephone in the hall and you feel uneasy about venturing into any of the rooms. While you are wondering what to do, you hear a noise coming from behind one of the doors. You rush back to the chair and sit down. Turn to **277**.

239

There are no hiding-places in the room. The bed is solid and reaches down to the floor. You appear to be safe. But suddenly your ears prick up as you hear a shuffling sound outside. Footsteps are approaching along the passageway. With ears peeled, you listen. The shuffling stops outside your door! Will you wait to see who is there (turn to **369**) or make other plans (turn to **281**)?

240

You manage to scramble to the door and slam it shut before the dogs can spring at you. Now out in the passageway, you must look for another way to leave this area. Turn to **60**.

241

The passageway you are in has rough stone walls and must run along the outside of the house. Rocky stairs lead downwards and you follow them until you reach the bottom. The air is cooler down here and you realize you must be in the cellars beneath the house. A half-hidden wooden door is standing ajar; you poke your head round it and peer into the room. Across the room is another door, but what you see in front of you fills you with alarm. Turn to **209**.

242

The boxes contain jewellery. Most of it is quite gaudy, but one ring in particular looks as though it might be valuable. It is a gold band with rubies inset around it. You bend over and hold it up to a candle to try to read an inscription running around the inside rim. It says: 'To dearest Margaret from George: 1834'. You may slip this into your pocket if you wish. Then turn to **290**.

243

A few steps further back down the passageway, two doors face each other. On the right is the Belial Room, which you may enter by turning to **312**. On the left is the Abaddon Room and you may try this door by turning to **335**. Otherwise you can continue round the passageway and walk downstairs (turn to **132**).

244

The Earl is outraged! How could you allow him to go to all the trouble of preparing a meal and then refuse to eat it? Will you apologize and take the duck (turn to **115**) or the lamb (turn to **196**), or will you apologize for the inconvenience, but still refuse to eat (turn to **96**)?

245

You bend down in the corner of the room to allow him to stand on your shoulders. Suddenly a thought occurs to you. Why has Rafferty not escaped already by standing on the table? You turn round to ask him – just in time to see his fist slam into your chin! You slump to the floor and Rafferty smiles. Capturing you will gain him the Master's favour once more. He has saved his own miserable hide, but you are about to be taken prisoner. You will spend the rest of your days beneath the House of Drumer until the Master tires of you.

246

You hear words coming from the old woman, yet her lips do not move. 'Stranger, how dare you invade the private bedchamber of the woman of the house?' she asks. You stammer an apologetic reply. She orders you: 'Begone, intruder. Leave an old woman to die in peace!'

lead downwards and you follow them until you reach the bottom. The air is cooler down here and you realize you must be in the cellars beneath the house. A half-hidden wooden door is standing ajar; you poke your head round it and peer into the room. Across the room is another door, but what you see in front of you fills you with alarm. Turn to **209**.

242

The boxes contain jewellery. Most of it is quite gaudy, but one ring in particular looks as though it might be valuable. It is a gold band with rubies inset around it. You bend over and hold it up to a candle to try to read an inscription running around the inside rim. It says: 'To dearest Margaret from George: 1834'. You may slip this into your pocket if you wish. Then turn to **290**.

243

A few steps further back down the passageway, two doors face each other. On the right is the Belial Room, which you may enter by turning to **312**. On the left is the Abaddon Room and you may try this door by turning to **335**. Otherwise you can continue round the passageway and walk downstairs (turn to **132**).

244

The Earl is outraged! How could you allow him to go to all the trouble of preparing a meal and then refuse to eat it? Will you apologize and take the duck (turn to **115**) or the lamb (turn to **196**), or will you apologize for the inconvenience, but still refuse to eat (turn to **96**)?

245

You bend down in the corner of the room to allow him to stand on your shoulders. Suddenly a thought occurs to you. Why has Rafferty not escaped already by standing on the table? You turn round to ask him – just in time to see his fist slam into your chin! You slump to the floor and Rafferty smiles. Capturing you will gain him the Master's favour once more. He has saved his own miserable hide, but you are about to be taken prisoner. You will spend the rest of your days beneath the House of Drumer until the Master tires of you.

246

You hear words coming from the old woman, yet her lips do not move. 'Stranger, how dare you invade the private bedchamber of the woman of the house?' she asks. You stammer an apologetic reply. She orders you: 'Begone, intruder. Leave an old woman to die in peace!'

Will you leave her as she wishes (turn to **159**) or ask her for information about the house (turn to **170**)?

247

Outside the study there are two doors in the hallway opposite each other. If you wish to try the door on the left, turn to **217**. If you would rather try the door on the right, turn to **307**. Otherwise you can continue along the hallway, following it round (turn to **316**).

248

You leave the torture room and can now continue along the passageway. Turn to **393**.

249

Slowly and quietly you walk up to the curtain. There is no movement from it. You grab the left-hand curtain and fling it open! There is a full-length window behind, which is barred on the outside. But nothing is hiding there. You take hold of the other curtain. But before you can move it, the bulges you noticed *come to life!* Turn to **236**.

250

You step up to a portrait of 'The Duchess of Brewster: 1777–1845'. She looks a stern old woman, with an icy stare; a lady of the nobility, no mistake. But as you stare, her image seems to shimmer. You blink, and try to look away. But you cannot! Within the shimmering face, you can see small movements and your jaw drops as the portrait's eyes turn towards you. Add 1 *FEAR* point for the fright. The woman's lips start to move and you hear a voice saying, 'Stranger, you have innocently stumbled into a cursed place. Would that I could bid you escape. But alas you cannot. There is evil and suffering within these walls and you may only escape by destroying it. But that is almost impossible. I can tell you this, though: you have an ally close by who may be able to help. This man is dressed in a grey robe. If you can find him, you may together free this house from the evil that controls it.' With these words, the shimmering stops. You rub your eyes and look again. The painting is still. Turn to **277**.

251

Across the hallway is another door. If you wish to try this door, turn to **97**. Otherwise you can turn right and follow the hallway (turn to **42**).

252

The corridor ends at a stout wooden door with Shaitan written on the name-plate. To your right is the Mammon room. And to your left is another door, but this one has no name. Do you wish to try any of these doors?

The Shaitan Room	Turn to **200**
The Mammon Room	Turn to **123**
The nameless door	Turn to **15**
Turn back and follow the landing	Turn to **272**

253

For fifteen minutes you try every loose brick in the hall. But you find nothing which will open the secret door. Perhaps that particular door can only be opened from the other wall. You must now choose your next plan. Will you go upstairs through the door at the top (turn to **293**) or look in the corner where the bats came from (turn to **165**)?

254

Your fears are confirmed when the door opens. The noise has attracted the attention of some mysterious friends of the Earl of Drumer. Four men enter the room, all dressed in white gowns and wearing goat's heads to conceal their faces. They are armed with knives and lengths of wood. It would be foolish to resist them. Grabbing your wrists, they take you downstairs into the cellars. There you enter a room in which there are four prison cells. Three are already occupied, but the fourth is empty. You will be detained here at the Earl's pleasure. Your adventure has ended.

255

You step out of the storeroom into a hallway. To your left, the hallway ends at a door which leads into the Shaitan room. If you wish to try the door, turn to **200**. Almost opposite is the Mammon room which you may enter by turning to **123**. If you are not interested in either of these, go back to the landing through the storeroom (turn to **233**).

256

You grab the vial boldly, remove the stopper and take a sip of the liquid inside. You wash it round your mouth to test the taste. It is thick and syrupy; not at all unpleasant. You swallow hard and wait with baited breath for it to take effect. For several moments nothing happens. Perhaps it will have no effect. You move over towards the cupboards and that is when you first notice a difference. Each step you take is an effort! Your feet feel like lead weights and your movements are sluggish. This liquid is a poison which saps the strength of those who take it. You must reduce your *SKILL* by 1 point and your *STAMINA* by 3. Continue by turning to **385**.

257

You consider your best plan as you walk down the passageway. You turn right along the landing and two doors are on your left. The first has Azazel written on its name-plate and the second, Mephisto. Do you want to try either of these rooms? If so you may enter the Azazel room by turning to **358** or the Mephisto room by turning to **298**. Otherwise you may pass both these rooms and walk along to where the landing turns right by turning to **287**.

258

'Escape?' he whimpers. 'You can only escape if the Master will allow it. But you have been kind to me. Yes, very kind. Shekou will help you leave. But the Master must not know. Please promise me that you will not tell the Master?' You agree and he leads you out of the room on to a landing. He points to a staircase across the landing. 'If you go down there, you will end up by the front door,' he says. 'The Master may have locked it, but I don't think so. Go. Quickly!' You walk cautiously round the landing towards the staircase. Shekou cannot walk as quickly as you and you leave him behind. You turn right and then right again. You are now across the landing from the Erasmus room and you look for the Hunchback. He has disappeared! You have passed a couple of rooms, but where has he gone? Is he letting the Master know of your whereabouts? Now you must decide what to do. Will you go downstairs (turn to **132**) or would you rather try a room nearby on the first floor (turn to **282**)?

259

The door is locked. You may either try the door across the hallway (turn to **118**) or go back along the hallway (turn to **49**).

260

The door is locked. You will not be able to go in. You turn and set off down the hallway. Will you enter a room on the right (turn to **113**) or will you carry on along the hallway (turn to **316**)?

261

You walk over to a corner where you can watch everything and catch your breath. You may add 4 *STAMINA* points for the rest. Now turn to **380**.

262

You climb into the bed and lie still. You can hear nothing, but then there is a single faint click as you shift your weight. You must have released a small catch, because you are suddenly flung upwards. Like a gigantic jaw, the bed has snapped up into the wall, swallowing you! It is pitch-black and the bed-clothes are thrown off you as you fly downwards for several metres before landing on something hard. Take 2 *STAMINA* points of damage and turn to **241**.

263

You step into a corner of the room and wait. The door opens slowly and a small, stocky man enters. His face is dumpy and dirty and he appears to be bent double. He squints into the room. Will you step forward and greet the man (turn to **367**) or leap across the room and attack (turn to **56**)?

264

You nurse your bruises and look around. All is pitch-black apart from a point of light coming from the end of a long tunnel. You walk down the tunnel cautiously and your pace slows even further when you hear the sound of voices in the distance. Human voices are chanting in a long, monotonous drone. Soon you are able to see what is happening. A group of people, perhaps forty of them, are gathered around a large fire. On the far side of the fire is an altar, and stretched out on the altar is a young woman. She is bound hand and foot. You cannot make out the faces of the onlookers, as they are all wearing goat-head masks. In the centre, standing over the altar, is a tall man dressed in robes, whose goat mask has been dyed purple. He holds in his hands a sharp dagger and is preparing to sacrifice his young victim. Do you wish to watch the proceedings (turn to **314**), try to find a way out (turn to **80**) or try to rescue the young woman (turn to **328**)?

265

'My humble apologies,' stammers the torturer. 'I did not realize you were one of my Master's brethren. Can I make amends? Can I help direct you onwards?' If you refuse his help, you may just leave the room (turn to **248**). If you want to ask the torturer how to get back upstairs, he will give you directions. If you follow them, you will end up back on the ground floor (turn to **293**).

266

The dark man courageously bares his chest and asks you to plunge a knife into his heart to end his suffering. If you have a knife, you can do as he wishes (turn to **182**) or you can refuse and talk to one of the other prisoners (turn to **143**).

267

The door opens wide and you are invited in. 'We thought everyone was here already,' says the older man. 'That's cutting it a bit fine. The others are. . .' He pauses when he sees your face and the two men look at each other. 'Er, ahem . . . what delayed you?' You are feeling a little uneasy about the situation and mumble some excuse about your car breaking down. 'Your car,' says the man slowly. 'What a shame – I hope it's not too bad.' From their reactions, you get the distinct impression that you have said the wrong thing. Then it dawns on you that there are no other cars around the house although, according to these two, everyone has arrived. You try desperately to think of what to say next and you do not notice that the younger man has crept round behind you. You feel a heavy blow on the back of your head, which knocks you unconscious. Lose 4 *STAMINA* points and turn to **173**.

268

'One of the Earl's servants?' he asks. 'I don't believe you. You don't look like one of his henchmen. *Who are you?*' Will you admit that you are an imposter (turn to **208**) or will you become angry and switch your story, pushing him out towards the door (turn to **127**)?

269

The wine is dry and light; obviously a very expensive vintage. But there is a puzzling aftertaste which you cannot place. Perhaps there is a little sediment in the decanter. No, the taste is more like ... *aspirin!* Too late, you realize that your wine has been drugged. You start to raise yourself from the table, but the effects are already taking hold. You stumble, fall back and crash to the floor. Consciousness fades. Turn to **173**.

270

You hurl the garlic at the Vampire and dash for the door. He shrieks, trying to brush off the garlic, as you fling it open. It opens into a cupboard – but a rather unusual one. The back wall has slid aside, revealing a secret passageway. The Vampire is rising to his feet again, so you decide to risk what lies ahead and step through into the passageway, slamming both doors behind you. Turn to **102**.

271

Continue your battle with him. If you win, you may either leave the room (turn to **378**) or check the table and the boxes (turn to **213**).

272

You follow the landing round, past a wooden door which bears the name Tuttivillus. You may try this door by turning to **155**. Straight ahead, the landing ends at a panelled wall and the passageway turns to the left. To follow the passage round, turn to **175**.

273

You collect your thoughts. The box! What is in the box that made it worth such a great deal of trouble? You pick it up and open it. Inside is a Golden Key. Do you now wish to leave the room (turn to **131**) or do you want to step through the mirror to see what lies behind (turn to **160**)?

274

You remove the stopper from the neck of the vial and sniff the contents. A strong, acrid odour hits your nostrils and you sneeze loudly and shake your head to drive away the smell. Quickly, you put the stopper back on the vial and too late, you see the sign etched into the glass. *A skull and crossbones!* You have sniffed a deadly poison which is now working its way through your system. You feel dizzy and the room starts to spin. Coughing violently, you slump to the floor. Consciousness fades as your last moments pass. But perhaps this is a merciful escape from the terrors of the House of Hell.

275

You grasp the rope and pull. From the depths of the house you hear a tinkling noise and the light coming from the side window goes out. Turn to **357**.

276

You feel around the wall, rapping the brick with your knuckles. Your heart leaps as you find a hollow area! You trace it with your fingers and the area is roughly the shape of a small door. Do you wish to look for a catch which will open the door (turn to **253**) or will you try a password (turn to **237**)?

His grip is strong and his eyes pierce yours

277

Footsteps! *Someone is coming!* The tall man you met earlier walks in, opening the door for another tall man dressed in a purple smoking-jacket. 'May I present Lord Kelnor, the Earl of Drumer,' the butler announces. The Earl holds out his hand and you shake it. His grip is strong and his eyes pierce yours. His lips widen to a soft smile. You begin to tell him of your predicament, but he holds up his hand. 'Please; I can see that you have been caught in this filthy storm. Let us sit by the fire and we will see whether we can help. Franklins, tell the cook to prepare some food for our visitor.' You protest that you do not wish to be any trouble, but your host ignores you and leads you into a drawing-room where a fire is burning. You take off your coat and sit down. The heat of the fire makes you feel comfortable once more. Franklins returns with two glasses of brandy. Will you relax, drink the brandy and ask if you can use the telephone (turn to **394**) or will you wait to see what he asks you (turn to **111**)?

278

Where will you try now? The door opposite (turn to **342**) or will you look for another way out of this corridor (turn to **60**)?

279

You turn to go the other way, but stop at the sound of definite footsteps coming along the corridor towards you. You must decide quickly what to do. Will you turn back and follow the Ghost into the room at the end of the corridor (turn to **73**) or take a chance and wait to see who is coming (turn to **142**)?

280

How many points did you score in total? If you scored 12 points or more, turn to **265**. If you scored 8-11 points, turn to **157**. If you scored less than 8 points, turn to **176**.

281

You can either step behind the door, ready to pounce on anything that comes through (turn to **369**), or you may try to hide from your visitor (turn to **203**).

282

You look over the landing and then turn round to consider your choices. There are two doors in front of you, both unmarked. If you wish to go through the door on the left, turn to **377**. If you wish to go through the door on the right, turn to **98**. If you would rather continue along the landing, turn to **374**.

283

'Before I will answer your question,' she says, 'you must tell me something – *what is my name?*' Do you know what her name is? If so, you will have noted down a reference number to turn to, should you be asked this question. Turn to this reference. If you do not know her name, she will not answer your question no matter what you threaten to do to her plants; you will have to leave the room by turning to **159**.

284

The Hunchback cringes as you strike him. 'Enough! Mercy! Please! I'll tell you the password! It is Pravemi. A member of the Earl's family, or something. Now leave me alone.' You step back from the miserable creature. Shekou scampers off through the door in the left-hand wall and leaves you alone. Will you walk on along the passage (turn to **393**) or would you prefer to explore the area around you (turn to **166**)?

285

The door is locked. You may either try the door opposite (turn to **353**) or creep back along the hallway (turn to **108**).

286

Another section of books is concerned with medieval portraits. You pull a large book down from the shelf. A book next to it falls over and reveals a small button set in the back of the bookcase. Do you wish to press this button? If so, turn to **225**. If not, you may look at the book you have chosen by turning to **311**.

287

You walk up to the two doors in the corner of the balcony. The one on your left is named Balthus and the one in front of you has no name. If you wish to enter the Balthus room, turn to **299**. If you would rather go through the other door, turn to **86**. If you choose to ignore these doors and continue round the landing, turn to **193**.

288

The Earl of Drumer drops to the floor, dead. You breathe a heavy sigh of relief, for you have defeated the evil Master of the House of Drumer. But what of Franklins? Must you also destroy the butler? Turn to **104**.

289

You walk from the porch round the side of the house. A light is indeed on, and it's shining through a window at the back of the building. Do you wish to go round to see if you can see anything at this window (turn to **345**) or will you walk up to one of the other windows along the side wall to see whether you can enter the house without anyone knowing (turn to **137**)?

290

You hear a rustling from the curtains and straighten up to look towards the window. You shudder with fright as the curtains open before you! Just as quickly, they shut again. Then there is silence. You walk slowly over and grab them! But they are perfectly ordinary curtains! You must add 1 *FEAR* point for the shock. Now do you wish to leave the room (turn to **2**) or will you try to work out the mystery of the curtains (turn to **150**)?

The man is tall and pale, with jet-black hair

291

In front of you is a high-backed armchair facing the fire, with its back towards you. A figure raises itself from the chair and turns to face you. The man is tall and pale, with jet-black hair. He wears a long black cape, fastened across the neck with a gold clasp. 'Yes,' he says, 'so far you have fared well against the occupants of the house. But I believe you will find that your run of luck has come to an end. Step forward so I can see you.' Will you step forward as he asks (turn to **326**) or will you prepare to attack the man (turn to **228**)?

292

You pour a measure of the deep brown liquid into one of the glasses and hold it up. It looks safe enough, so you take a sip. *Delicious!* The brandy warms you inside as it slips down and you may add 3 *STAMINA* points. You spy a hip-flask on a shelf in one corner and you may take some of the brandy with you if you wish. Now you can look around the room. Do you wish to examine the corner shelf where you found the hip-flask (turn to **192**) or the fireplace and the mantelpiece (turn to **303**), or will you leave this drawing-room (turn to **218**)?

293

You open the door at the top of the stairs. Facing you is a door, and to your right the hallway ends at another door. Do you wish to enter the door opposite (turn to **113**), the door to your right (turn to **260**) or turn left into a main hallway (turn to **316**)?

294

The door is locked. If you have any keys with you, you may try them in the lock. Do you have a Golden Key? If so, you can try it by turning to **10**. If not, turn to **204**.

295

'Secret rooms?' she laughs. 'Why this house is riddled with secret passageways and secret rooms. Most are in the cellar though, but some of the upstairs passages lead to them. The most cunning secret room is the Master's most trusted hiding-place. It can only be reached by one way, and that is from under the stairs in the cellar. A password is needed and I knew the old one, but it has recently been changed. Shekou will know the new password...' The woman's eyes close, as if the conversation has been a great strain. You leave her be and consider the information you have been given. When you are in a position to find the secret door in question (under the cellar stairs), you may try to find it by *deducting 10 from the reference you will be on at the time, and turning to the new reference.* No other clue as to its location will be given. But first you must find the password! Leave the room by turning to **159**.

296

The key turns and the door opens. You step into the dining-room. The long table is set for two with fine silver. A sparkling chandelier, festooned with candles, lights the room. The walls are covered with plush red wallpaper. Full-length curtains are drawn along one of the walls. You are prepared for your battle. A rope hangs down by the curtains. You can pull this, if you wish, to ring for the butler (turn to **318**). Otherwise you can check round the room for signs of any traps (turn to **185**).

297

Score the points indicated for any of the following choices:

Mammon	3 points
Man in white	2 points
Mordana	5 points
Man in grey	2 points

You score no points for any other selection. Now turn to **141**.

The handle turns and the door opens a little, but it is caught on something and will not open any further. Do you wish to try to force the door (turn to **390**) or will you leave it and continue along the landing (turn to **287**)?

The room you have entered is bare. Pin-striped wallpaper covers the wall. A hearth is set in the centre of one wall and on the mantelpiece there is a small wooden box. Curtains are pulled together along another wall, but they hang awkwardly, bulging at unnatural places. Do you wish to:

Investigate the bulging curtains?	Turn to **249**
Open the box on the mantelpiece?	Turn to **197**
Leave the room?	Turn to **152**

300

'Ha!' he laughs, continuing to advance as you back towards the window. 'All right, then. If you really are not one of the Master's brethren, *make the sign of the cross!* You consider this harmless request. You touch your forehead, then your chest, then each shoulder, and look back at him. His eyes open wide. 'It is true!' he exclaims. 'You really are an outsider! Oh, my friend, how can you forgive me for my inexcusable attack? How was I to know? For none of the Master's followers would dare to cross themselves!' You tell him that you accept his apologies and ask him whether he can help you. Do you wish to ask him how you can escape from the house (turn to **75**) or how you may defeat the Master (turn to **105**)?

301

Although you defeat their leader, you cannot hold off the other three men, who surround and capture you. One of them runs off to get the keys to the cells. When he returns you are locked into the fourth cell. Your adventure ends here...

302

You spring on the Hunchback and attack. Resolve your battle:

HUNCHBACK   *SKILL 7*   *STAMINA 7*

If you win, you may either head for the staircase (turn to **393**) or explore the cellar (turn to **166**).

303

A fine carriage-clock sits in the centre of an elaborately carved wooden mantelpiece. A number of letters are jammed in behind the clock and you reach for them. As you do so, your sleeve catches one of the carved images in the woodwork and it moves! You lean forward to examine it. It is a small carved demonic face which can be moved sideways. Do you wish to see what lies behind the wooden face (turn to **85**) or will you read through the letters (turn to **364**)?

304

Three portraits are particularly interesting. Will you look at a beautiful young woman wearing a tiara (turn to **151**), a middle-aged, portly gentleman wearing half-moon glasses (turn to **37**) or an elderly woman with grey hair and a cold expression (turn to **250**)?

305

The door has a bolt on the outside. You undo the bolt and open the door, peering cautiously into the room. The walls are bare and it is sparsely furnished, with only a table and chair. Sitting in a corner asleep is a man in a white gown. As you open the door he wakes with a start. 'Oh, hello!' he says. 'I suppose you've come for me, have you?' Will you say yes (turn to **127**) or no (turn to **153**)?

306

The door is firmly locked. You will not enter the house this way. If you wish, you can knock at the door to try to attract the attention of the two men who were talking. If you decide to do this, you must *Test your Luck*. If you are Lucky, they will hear you and come to investigate (turn to **190**). If you are Unlucky, they are out of earshot and you will not get through this way. If you decide against knocking at the door, or if you have been Unlucky, you will have to go back to the front door and either knock (turn to **357**) or pull the bell-pull (turn to **275**).

307

You try the handle. It turns; the door is unlocked, but the sound of voices puts you on your guard. You inch the door open and look through the crack. It reveals an elegant room with a polished wooden floor. At one end is an enormous full-length mirror. You can see the rest of the room reflected in this mirror. A mural, depicting a tranquil country scene, covers the wall facing the mirror. The reflection shows the room to be empty, apart from a table and chairs in the centre of the floor, but you can definitely hear voices coming from inside the room. This is all very puzzling, but you decide against entering the room when one of the voices calls out, 'Who's that at the door?' Instead you decide to leave quickly! Will you go through the door opposite (turn to **217**) or nip along the hallway (turn to **316**)?

308

'The people?' he asks. 'Ah, yes, the *people*. Of course. Tonight is the night. There are many people here. The Master is holding a special occasion tonight and his friends are here. All are friends of the Master. That is, all except the one in grey. For he has betrayed the Master's trust and he will be punished. Yes, punished, before the night is out. The Master put him in the Asmodeus room – and he's promised to let me watch. But you have nothing to fear if you are a friend of the Master. You *are* a friend of the Master, aren't you? Perhaps he'll let you watch, too!' The Hunchback is giggling with glee at the thought of the night's activities. You have gained all the useful information you will get out of him, so you leave the room, locking him in. Turn to **350**.

309

The dining-room looks magnificent. A long table stretches between two fine chairs and is laid with gleaming silvery cutlery. A rich red wallpaper covers the walls and the room is lit by a sparkling chandelier, bristling with candles, which hangs from the ceiling. You take your seat and the butler moves behind you to offer you wine. Will you take white wine (turn to **269**) or red (turn to **395**)?

310

If you wish to look for secret doors, turn to **276**. Otherwise, return to the last reference and choose again.

311

The book contains a collection of portraits of the nobility painted many centuries ago. It is undoubtedly worth a small fortune. You may take it with you if you wish, then leave the study by turning to **54**.

312

You enter the room and study its contents. It seems that this room is used very little and is perhaps a storeroom. White sheets are covering the furniture and several large, square shapes which look like boxes. Do you wish to rest here (turn to **261**) or look under the sheets to see what they are hiding (turn to **167**)?

313

The man hesitates and eyes you suspiciously. You tell him you mean him no harm and that you are only looking for a way out of the house. 'Fool!' he screams. 'Do you expect me to believe your feeble lies? You are one of *them*. And if *they* are to punish me, they will find that I will not give in without a fight!' With these words he advances towards you. Do you wish to:

Try to persuade him that
you are not one of *them*?   Turn to **34**
Ask him how you can convince
him that he is wrong?   Turn to **300**
Spring at him quickly to
get in the first blow?   Turn to **271**

314

The pitch increases as the onlookers join hands and circle the altar. The priest raises his knife into the air. and lets out a frenzied scream as he brings it down. You force yourself to look away and suddenly, you notice another passageway leading off from the room. You look back at the gathering. They are all busy with the sacrifice, smearing the unfortunate victim's blood all over themselves. You seize your opportunity and run for the passage. *Test your Luck.* If you are Lucky, turn to **129**. If you are Unlucky, turn to **187**.

315

'All right, Orville, that will do for now,' says the torturer. He turns to you. Have you been convincing enough for him? Over the next five references, some of the answers that he would have been expecting are listed. Each one scores a number of points. If you choose one of the words listed, record how many points you score. When you have been through all five references, you will have convinced the torturer if your score is high enough. Now turn to **235**.

316

Two doors face each other across the hallway just before it ends at a wall. Do you want to try the door on the left (turn to **205**) or the door on the right (turn to **118**)?

317

You cut yourself free and massage your wrists to get the circulation moving again. Then you walk over to the door to try it. It is not locked! You try the handle, open it a little, and look outside. Your room is on a first-floor landing. Facing the door is a balustrade, and looking over the banisters you can see the entrance hall below. To your left, there are two doors in the corner of the landing, which runs along to the right. If you wish to go this way, turn to **287**. Looking to your right, the landing runs past another door and then turns to the left. To go this way, turn to **33**.

They step apart and advance round the table towards you

318

A few moments later, Franklins, the butler, enters the dining-room. He is startled to see you. You demand to talk to the master of the house and he agrees to pass on your request. Ten minutes later, the Earl of Drumer comes storming angrily into the room, with Franklins following close behind. They stand facing you across the table, watching you carefully. 'Why have I been disturbed in the middle of the night?' he demands. You tell him that you know of the evil that goes on in the house and that you are determined to destroy it. The two men look at each other, they nod and look back at you, then they step apart and advance round the table towards you, the Earl to your left and his butler to your right. You must choose quickly whom you will attack first. If you fight the Earl first, turn to **30**. If you attack Franklins first, turn to **351**.

319

The butler brings in a plate of cheese and a steaming pot of coffee. He cuts you a portion of cheese and pours your coffee into a china cup. The conversation continues. Turn to **74**.

320

You shelter under the stairs and fend off the bats with your hands. They soon discover that they cannot get at you while you are tucked away; and they flap off back to the corner from which they came. When all is quiet again, you may decide your next move. Will you head up the stairs and open the door at the top (turn to **293**) or will you remain to explore the bats' chamber (turn to **330**)?

321

'Before I will answer your question,' she says, 'you must tell me something – *what is my name?*' Do you know what her name is? If so, you will have noted a reference number to turn to, should you be asked this question. Turn to this reference. If you do not know her name, she will not answer your question no matter what you threaten to do to her plants, and you will have to leave the room by turning to **159**.

322

The girl is hysterical. It seems that she is a district nurse who has just been assigned to the area. She knocked on the door, was invited in and then captured. She pleads with you to help her and her voice rises to a scream. But what can you do? The keys to the cells are nowhere to be seen. You begin to get worried that her hysterics may attract the attentions of the occupants of the house and you try to calm her down. Do you want to talk to one of the others as well (turn to **143**) or will you leave the room quickly (turn to **91**)?

323

The door is locked. The handle and lock are part of an ornate metal plate. Do you have a cast-iron key with you? If so, deduct the number on the key from this reference number and turn to the resulting reference to open the door. Otherwise, you must try the door opposite – and quickly, because you can hear footsteps approaching from the hallway. Turn to **118**.

324

The underside of the table forms a closed box, and this arouses your suspicions. You knock on it. It is hollow. Perhaps it is a secret compartment? You feel around underneath and, sure enough, your fingers find a small catch which releases a hidden drawer. Inside this drawer is a leather box. But wait! What is that noise? You can hear footsteps outside the door. You will have to hide quickly. Will you grab the case and take it with you (turn to **147**) or will you leave it behind and close the drawer (turn to **100**)?

325

'What is happening?' he asks. 'But surely you know. Is that not why you are here? Tonight Brother Isaacson is to receive the Master's blessing.' Your quizzical look takes the Hunchback by surprise. He realizes he's said the wrong thing. 'You are not one of the Master's friends, are you? A curse on me. I should have realized,' he moans. 'The Master will punish me for this. I must warn him!' He hobbles towards the door to try to escape, but you are too quick for him. You force him out of the way and spring outside the room, locking the door behind you. Turn to **350**.

326

The tall man spreads his cloak. He is staring directly into your eyes and his dark pupils seem to pierce your mind. At the last minute you panic and try to break his gaze, but it is no use. You are under his control. He covers you with his cape and your last memory is a sharp stab as his teeth sink into your neck.

327

You step over to the back door and grasp the handle. The

handle turns, but the door will not open. It is locked and the key is nowhere about – or is it? Do you want to grab the bunch of keys on the cooker (turn to **148**) or try the other door (turn to **126**)?

328

You leap into the centre of the ceremony with a loud war-cry. The young woman looks up at you hopefully. Your daring rescue is commendable for its bravery, but unbelievably stupid. For how can you hope to stand your ground against forty opponents. They surround you, grab you and the priest cuts your throat with his knife. You deserved to die!

329

Outside the Belial room you have two options. Do you wish to try the Abaddon room across the way (turn to **335**) or would you rather now head to the staircase and creep downstairs (turn to **132**)?

330

Where do you wish to look?

In the corner from which the bats came?	Turn to **165**
Along the back wall?	Turn to **356**
Under the stairs?	Turn to **61**

A faint, white figure has appeared in front of you

331

Although you fight the power that draws you to the book, its force is greater than your resistance. Gradually your will is overcome. As you collapse on the floor, your spirit is sucked out of your body and into the eye. Like the other weak-willed victims who have already come under the book's power, you are doomed to an eternal life of agony trapped within the pupil of the Hypnotic Eye.

332

At the end of the corridor ahead of you is a stout wooden door. While you are considering whether or not to try this room, a noise behind you startles you. You spin round, only to find that the wind is rustling wall-hangings; there is nothing to be afraid of. You turn back, and are amazed to find a faint, white figure has appeared in front of you! This apparition is a young woman in her early twenties, with long flowing hair. She is dressed in a white bridal dress which has seen better days; it is ripped and torn. 'Oh, thank God I have found you in time!' she says. 'I must talk to you immediately! Come, let us go into this room.' Will you follow her into the room (turn to **73**) or do you suspect a trap and would rather turn back (turn to **279**)? Whichever you choose, you must add 1 *FEAR* point for your encounter.

333

Orville is now getting the hang of this game and is enjoying himself. M is his next letter. Write immediately or lose another *STAMINA* point. Then turn to **76**.

334

Your cold stare frightens the man. I see you really are one of the Master's loyal friends,' he whimpers. 'I, er... I merely suggested that to make sure I was talking to an honourable person. I expect my time has come, has it?' He looks at you pitifully and drops to his knees. Again you merely glare at him silently. Suddenly he reacts! Before you can stop him, he has pulled a short dagger from his robe and, with both hands, has plunged it into his stomach! You watch, horrified, as the man slumps to the floor, face downwards. Any knowledge that you could have gained from him has now been lost. You curse silently and leave the room. Turn to **278**.

335

You enter a bedroom which is lit by a single candle burning by the bedside. A heavy, musty odour hangs in the air, which could come from all the plants which are standing in pots on the mantelpiece, bedside table, dresses and shelves. Whoever used this room certainly liked plants! But another sight catches your attention; and stops you in your tracks, Asleep in the bed is an old woman! It seems that she has not heard you, for she has not moved since you entered the room. Do you wish to leave her in peace (turn to **159**), walk over and wake her (turn to **139**) or will you instead spring over and attack her before she can wake (turn to **354**)?

336

You catch up with the butler in the corner of the room. Resolve your fight with him and, if you are attacking with the Kris dagger, add 3 points to your *SKILL* during the battle:

FRANKLINS   *SKILL 8*   *STAMINA 8*

When you have inflicted your first wound on Franklins, turn to **181**.

337

You walk over to the mantelpiece and study the trinkets scattered along it. A couple of lacquer boxes and a picture-frame (with no picture) flank a large plant-pot with a broad-bladed plant growing in it. In the grate below are several lumps of coal resting on a bed of paper – a fire all ready to light. But something else is in the grate. A black-and-white photograph has been thrown on to the coals. Do you wish to check the contents of the boxes (turn to **242**) or pick up the photograph to look at it (turn to **199**)?

338

The bedside table catches your attention; particularly the silver tray. Laid out on it is a bedtime snack of bread, jam and tea. You examine it carefully and decide it should be safe enough. You sit down on the bed and help yourself. It is delicious! You may add 4 *STAMINA* points and 1 *LUCK* point for this find. When you are ready, leave the room by turning to **243**.

339

You are standing by two doors, and each has a name-plate. Ahead of you is the Asmodeus room. You may try this door by turning to **154**. To your right is the Eblis room, which you can enter by turning to **125**; or you can follow the corridor until it turns left by turning to **252**.

340

You feel around on the floor, but come across only earth and straw. A shuffling at the door reminds you of the visitor approaching. Turn to **263**.

341

At the end of the bench is a rack which holds four glass vials, and each vial contains a coloured liquid. They look like the results of someone's experiment. Are you willing to risk taking a sip of one of these liquids? If so, which colour will you choose:

Green?	Turn to **149**
Red?	Turn to **274**
Clear?	Turn to **256**
Yellow?	Turn to **161**

If this seems a little too dangerous, you may instead look through the drawers (turn to **81**) or the cupboards (turn to **371**).

342

The door is not locked, but the shufflings and yelpings that you can hear inside suggest that you ought to proceed with caution. Will you decide against entering and examine the passageway you are in (turn to **60**), or will you fling the door open wide and stride boldly in (turn to **14**)?

343

Fight the bats as a single creature:

BATS   *SKILL 4*   *STAMINA 4*

If you defeat the bats, you may either climb the stairs and open the door at the top (turn to **293**), or you can explore the bats' chamber (turn to **330**).

344

The door is firmly locked. Whoever is in there doesn't want to be disturbed. Will you now open the door on the right-hand wall (turn to **209**) or press on (turn to **91**)?

345

The lit window is next to a back door which leads into a kitchen. Voices are coming from the kitchen, but you cannot see anyone. Whoever is in there must be standing by the back wall, out of sight. You strain to hear what is being said. There appear to be two people in the kitchen, and they are talking excitedly. '. . .Master is getting ready. I'm starting to get excited. I've never been to one before. Do you really think we may be *visited?*' Another man's voice, rather more controlled, replies: 'You know, I'm having doubts about this whole affair. She is so young and she came here in all innocence. I just don't know.' The two men walk around the kitchen and you can see them more clearly. They are both dressed in white gowns. One is a good deal younger than the other. Do you wish to knock on the door to see whether they will let you in (turn to **207**), or will you wait and listen for a little longer (turn to **68**)?

346

How will you try to escape? You must go back down the corridor and turn right. But will you proceed cautiously, ready to nip into the rooms you pass if you hear anyone (turn to **257**), or will you race for the staircase and run back downstairs (turn to **132**)?

347

The Hunchback has had enough of your chat and turns to go through the door on the left. He points down the passageway, saying, 'Head on down here for the stairs.' Turn to **91**.

348

You force yourself free from the pillow and leap out of bed, gasping. Was it just your imagination, or were the bedclothes really trying to suffocate you? In any case, you decide that you are definitely not welcome in this room. You get dressed and walk out of the room back on to the landing. Turn to **121**.

349

You wait until there is silence in the drawing-room and step carefully back through the mirror into the room. The coast is clear. You walk over to the door and leave the room. Turn to **131**.

350

You are on a landing overlooking the entrance hall. To your right, the passageway ends at a door. To the left, the landing turns right past a couple of doors.

Do you wish to turn to the right (turn to **332**), or would you prefer to follow the landing round to the left (turn to **257**)?

351

You turn towards the butler. He stops and takes a step backwards; you step forwards. Franklins runs round to the other side of the table. 'Franklins!' screams the Earl. 'Move in, man! Step up and attack!' The butler twitches nervously. Will you continue pursuing him (turn to **336**) or will you leave the cowardly butler for the time being and concentrate on the Earl (turn to **30**)?

352

'Next letter, Orville!' shouts the torturer. Orville thinks, and says: 'A'. Write down your answer straight away or lose a point of *STAMINA*. Then turn to **57**.

The door opens into a large, but cosy, drawing-room. The dying embers of a warm fire burn in the hearth. Comfortable chairs are arranged around the fireplace. Two glasses and a decanter stand on a glass-topped table between the chairs. There are plants in tall stands on either side of the windows, and there is another door next to the one you came in. Do you wish to explore the room further (turn to **119**), leave through the other door (turn to **218**) or will you have a little tipple from the decanter (turn to **292**)?

354

You creep over to the bedside. She does not move. You raise your hands over your head, ready to strike. You take a deep breath and tense your muscles. . . *Her eyes flick open!* She stares vacantly up into the air with milky-white eyes and the sight makes you shudder with horror. *Her blank eyes have no pupils! A* cold sweat breaks out on your brow and your hands drop to your sides impotently. You must add 3 *FEAR* points for the shock. Will you turn and run through the door back into the passageway (turn to **159**) or wait to see what happens next (turn to **246**)?

355

You grope around in the blackness and find nothing. If you wish, you may *Test your Luck* – if you are Lucky turn to **50**; if you are Unlucky turn to **340**. Otherwise you can wait to see whether the approaching figure will be able to help you (turn to **263**).

356

You feel along the wall for any sign of a secret entrance, but find nothing. Just as you are beginning to think you are wasting your time, your left hand dislodges a brick. Behind the brick is a lever. You pull the lever and a rumbling noise comes from the wall near by. A section of the wall slides to one side, revealing a small entrance just large enough for you to climb through. You look inside, but it is pitch-black. Do you want to step through this doorway (turn to **387**) or would you rather not risk it and climb the stairs instead (turn to **293**)?

A crude scientific laboratory of some sort

357

A few moments later, the door-handle turns slowly and the door opens. Standing in the doorway is a tall man dressed in a dark suit with tails. His long face is solemn. 'Yes?' he asks, indignantly. You smile nervously and explain your situation. Your car has broken down, you need to reach a telephone and you are soaked to the skin. The man's face remains expressionless. 'Come in,' he orders. 'The Master is expecting you. Follow me.' He leads you into a reception hall and tells you to sit down while he informs his master of your arrival. Turn to **8**.

358

The door opens and you peer into the room. You quickly check that there is no one inside and are relieved to find it's empty – but full of clutter. It seems to be a crude scientific laboratory of some sort. A brass telescope points through the window towards the sky. Charts and mathematical tables are pinned to the walls. A human skeleton hangs from a hook, and a bench is covered with glass vials and apparatus. They look like priceless antiques, and they were probably all made in the last century. Do you wish to investigate the room further (turn to **117**), or would you prefer to leave (turn to **11**)?

359

You explain that you have no wish to kill him and he steps back, puzzled. 'Do you mean you're not one of the coven? You're an outsider?' You nod. An elated expression spreads across his face. Turn to **208**.

360

You grit your teeth and shove your bound hands against the window-pane, rope first. Your first blow is not hard enough to break the glass, so you try again. This time the glass shatters and some large pieces fall on to the floor. But your desperate action does not leave you unhurt. You receive a nasty gash on your left wrist. Deduct 2 *STAMINA* points and turn to **317**.

361

You pull the garlic out of your pocket and hold it up before the man. His expression changes from one of confidence to a look of fright. As you suspected, this

VAMPIRE cannot bear to be near raw garlic. Sweat breaks out on his forehead and he backs off towards the bed. He is heading for one of the other doors in the room. You hurriedly look round, trying to decide the best way out. Will you try the door on the left (turn to **189**), the door on the right, which he was heading for (turn to **270**), or will you turn round and dash quickly for the door you came in through (turn to **90**)?

362

You taste the liquid. It is white wine! You drink some more and it warms you. You start to feel a little light-headed and dizzy; then suddenly you feel a stab of pain in your stomach and you double over. But there is no relief from this pain, because you have drunk a bottle of poisoned wine! In a few moments you will lose consciousness and in five minutes you will be dead. You will never make tomorrow's appointment after all...

363

You step up to the balding man's cell. 'Do not waste your time in here,' he says, 'for you cannot help us. Our only hope is that you can destroy the evil in this house before it destroys us. But that is unlikely, because you would have to destroy the Master first. He may only be killed with the Kris knife and the battle may only take place in a *red* room – to symbolize a battle taking place in hell itself. The dining-room upstairs has red walls, but it is always locked and the key is hidden behind the mirror when ceremonies are taking place. If you can find the Kris knife and the key, then you may save the world from the devilry that is brewing within these walls. But as for *us,* we will all be dead before the night is out. Don't waste your time with us.' You listen to his advice and consider whether you ought to leave immediately, as he suggests (turn to **91**) or whether you should talk to the others (turn to **143**).

364

The letters are not particularly interesting except for one from a foreign address, written in immaculate handwriting with a broad-nibbed black pen. It is addressed to the Earl of Drumer and appears to warn him of possible dangers. It starts by describing a raid of some sort on the writer's house and how he narrowly escaped being caught. It ends with a P.S. which says: 'I also suggest you further protect yourself by changing the password on your own *cache* room. I for one know it is Goathead. How many others know the same? Why not change it to something which will remind you of the sound advice of a good friend?' The letter is signed by 'Count Pravemi'. You read this through again and replace the letter. Do you now wish to leave the room (turn to **218**) or will you turn your attention back to the small wooden face on the mantelpiece (turn to **85**)?

365

You put up a good fight, but the sheer numbers of the devil-worshippers overwhelm you. You are captured and will remain so until you feel the priest's knife on the sacrificial altar – for you will be the next victim.

366

You head back down the corridor until you reach the stairs again. The passageway runs past the stairs and you decide to continue this way. A little further along you come to a small flight of stairs; but the passageway is so dark that you do not notice them in time. You tumble down and land in a heap at the bottom. Lose 1 *STAMINA* point. Turn to **264**.

367

You cough lightly and step forward. The man turns towards you and jumps back, startled. You apologize for frightening him and explain your situation. He eyes you suspiciously and calms down, saying: 'Of course I'll help you! Er, ahem ... follow me.' As he turns and walks through the door you can see that he is not bent over double, but has a hunched back. You follow him from the room. Turn to **210**.

368

There is nothing of interest in the cupboards. You may now leave the room by turning to **243**.

369

You watch the door-handle cautiously, preparing yourself for whoever or *whatever* should appear. The handle turns ... and then it's released. The shuffling noise disappears down the passageway. Your visitor has decided to leave this room alone! Breathing a sigh of relief, you sit down on the bed. But what will your next plan be? Would you like to take a short nap and perhaps gain some *STAMINA* (turn to **262**) or would you rather leave the room and either follow the passage round (turn to **252**) or return to the landing (turn to **272**)?

370

The bats claw at you as you run up the stairs, but you manage to reach the top without any serious wounds. Deduct 1 *STAMINA* point for the cuts and scratches. At the top of the stairs is a door. Light shines under the door and frightens the bats away. You may open it, but be careful to do so slowly. Turn to **293**.

371

You step over to the cupboards and try the doors. They are not locked. You grasp the handles and open the cupboard doors wide. Just as quickly, you slam them shut! Shaking nervously, you step away, holding your hands up to your gaping mouth. For the sight inside has given you a terrible shock, and you must add 2 *FEAR* points. Hanging from hooks inside the cupboards are two corpses which have evidently been used for experiments of some kind. The blood has not yet dried on these corpses – and they are still warm! You lean back against the bench to compose yourself. Turn to **385**.

A man shuffles into the room

372

You sit on the bed, trying to work out how on earth you can escape from this place. The room you are now in seems safe enough and the rest refreshes you – add 2 *STAMINA* points. But a few moments later, the wind whistling through the curtains attracts your attention. You glance over towards the window. Turn to **168**.

373

The door opens slowly and a man shuffles into the room carrying a glass containing a clear liquid. He appears to be bent double and his movements are slow. As he gets nearer to the bed, you realize he will soon notice that you are not there. Do you want to nip out of the room quickly and lock the door behind you (turn to **350**) or will you leap on the man and attack him (turn to **399**)?

374

The landing turns right and a passage branches off. You may either turn left down the passageway and past a couple of doors before turning left again (turn to **339**); or turn right, following the landing (turn to **272**).

375

You step back up to the fireplace and examine the secret button again. Will you press it (turn to **392**) or will you leave the drawing-room (turn to **218**)?

376

You glance at the bed and an idea dawns on you. Perhaps you could hide under the bedclothes – there is nowhere else in the room to hide. If you wish to try this, turn to **262**. Otherwise turn to **369**.

377

You step into a small storeroom and close the door behind you. There are shelves on the left and right walls, on which various household objects are stored. In front of you, in the wall facing the door, is *another* door. What do you want to do? Will you search through the things on the shelves (turn to **83**), try the door opposite (turn to **255**) or return to the landing (turn to **233**)?

378

The hallway outside is clear. You decide against turning right and following the passageway, which is a dead end. You may enter the Eblis room to your immediate left (turn to **125**) or you may continue back towards the landing and follow it (turn to **272**).

379

You still find no signs of any traps. Ring for the butler by turning to **318**.

380

You keep a suspicious eye on the room while you consider your next move. Suddenly, one of the sheets flaps. Was it the wind? No, you think, the air is perfectly still. You watch the sheet. Slowly, it rises into the air as if it was being pulled up on a rope! Add 1 *FEAR* point and decide quickly what to do. Will you grab the sheet (turn to **70**) or leave the room and slam the door firmly behind you (turn to **329**)?

381

'Right, then!' says the torturer. 'Let's see if you really do know the Master or not. Orville here will give you a letter. You tell me the first word that comes into your head beginning with that letter. If you take your time and think too long about your answer, Dirk will tighten the rack. Got that? All right, let's start.' Each time the torturer's assistant gives you a letter, you must write down on a piece of paper the first word you can think of which begins with that letter and relates to the house. After your test is complete, the torturer will consider your answers and then decide whether or not he believes your story. To start (when you have pencil and paper ready), turn to **38**.

382

You leave the Diabolus room and are standing once more in the narrow corridor outside. Do you wish to turn left to investigate the window (turn to **110**) or would you rather return to the landing and follow it round (turn to **193**)?

383

You step back from the battle, nurse your wounds and look at the eight dead bodies on the floor. You shake your head at the senseless waste of life. Searching round the room, you find nothing of any value. But if you are thirsty, there is a jug of water in one corner of the room. Presumably this is drinking-water for the dogs. You may drink from it if you wish. If you do, you may gain 2 *STAMINA* points if your *STAMINA* score was less than 12. If it was more than 12, you will gain no *STAMINA* points, as you were not thirsty. You decide to leave the room and explore the passageway outside. Turn to **60**.

384

You pull out a heavy book with a large eye embossed on the spine. The cover has no title and you flick the book open. The frontispiece is an elaborately detailed drawing of a symbolic eye. You cannot help staring at the illustration and, as you do so, the dark pupil seems to glint as if it were made of glass. Shapes start to appear and faint sounds reach your ears. The sounds are screams of agony! The shapes in the eye are contorted human faces racked with pain! You shiver with fright as you look at the poor wretches, and you must add 2 *FEAR* points. Realizing what is happening, you try to close the book, but something is compelling you to keep on staring at the eye. Roll two dice and compare the total with your *SKILL* score. If your roll exceeds your skill, turn to **331**. Otherwise turn to **39**.

385

Suddenly your ears prick up at the sound of footsteps coming closer. You nip into the shadows and wait. The footsteps stop outside the door and you can hear two voices talking: 'Hadn't we better ask the Master's permission?' one asks. 'Hmm. Maybe you're right. And we'd better get a light for the lamps.' You breathe a sigh of relief as the footsteps disappear off in the direction you approached the room. You decide it is best to leave before they return and you open the door on to the landing. The safest way to go, it strikes you, is away from the two visitors, who may return at any moment. If you approached this room from the left, turn to **229**; if you came from the right, turn to **26**.

386

You clear your throat and call out softly; you certainly don't want to disturb anyone else in the house. There is no reply. You step forwards, stumble over a chamber-pot and crash to the floor. That's strange, you think – surely you would have seen right in front of you. You rise to your feet and wince. You have banged your knee badly. Deduct 2 *STAMINA* points and turn to **290**.

A hubbub of voices grows louder as a group of
people come towards the room

387

You find yourself in a dark tunnel. It is quite short, and ends at a door. You open the door slowly and, when you are sure there is no one inside, you step into the room. It seems to be some sort of ceremonial ante-room or dressing-room. Hanging from hooks around the walls are thirty to forty white gowns, and resting on shelves underneath the gowns are macabre masks, made from goats' heads. A single passageway leads off to the left. While you are wondering where to go next, a sound sends a chill down your spine. *Someone is coming!* A hubbub of voices grows louder as a group of people come towards the room. You look quickly round for somewhere to hide and decide to nip behind the door. Suddenly the door opens and about forty people come into the room, all chattering excitedly. You mingle with them and merge unnoticed into the crowd. They are ribbing a man called Brother Isaacson. It seems that tonight is a very significant night for him. You copy what they are doing, laughing and smiling, and even getting dressed up in a gown and mask. Eventually, when they are dressed, they all move off along the other passageway. Will you go along with them (turn to **122**) or will you hang around at the back, hoping to stay behind unnoticed in the room (turn to **219**)?

388

'Before I will answer your question,' she says, 'you must tell me something – what is my name?' Do you know what her name is? If so, you will have noted down a reference number to turn to, should you be asked this question. Turn to this reference. If you do not know her name, she will not answer your question no matter what you threaten to do to her plants and you must leave the room by turning to **159**.

389

You step into the passageway and follow the hall round to the right; back to where it rejoins the landing. You carry straight on. Turn to **272**.

390

You heave the door with your shoulder. The wood creaks and it opens a little further; enough to let you into the room. It is small and bare; and a cold, damp wind swirls through it, billowing the curtains. The window pane is smashed and the floor beneath the window is sodden from the rain. You look around, but there is nothing unusual in the room, apart from a frayed length of knotted rope. You may take this with you if you wish and leave. As you pull the door to you find a piece of glass wedged underneath it, which was making it stick. You turn left out of the room and continue along the landing. Turn to **287**.

391

You race across to the door and twist the handle. *Aaaaah!* You stifle a scream and release the handle immediately as an electric shock runs up your arm. Lose 2 *STAMINA* points and turn to **277**.

392

You press the button and hear a small click. Then you hear another sound and you swing round to face the corner shelf. Beside this shelf, a sliding panel has opened in the wall. You walk over to investigate and bend down to look at the opening. Too late, you realize that the panel has revealed, not a tunnel at all, but a false opening. The wall behind is solid. But it has served its purpose: you have been lured into a trap! You are standing on a trap-door which opens beneath you and you fall downwards. Turn to **397**.

393

The passageway widens into a small chamber. Although it is dark, you can see a staircase going up a few metres ahead of you. To your right, the chamber opens out into a wide area. You step forwards and, almost immediately, a twittering noise puts you on your guard. Suddenly you feel something land on your head and dig sharp claws into your scalp! You gasp and swat it away. Your hand touches a small, leathery body and a pair of wings start to flap as it rises from your head. BATS! A number of them are flapping around your head, darting and scratching with their claws. You must add 1 *FEAR* point for the shock. Do you wish:

To run up the stairs?	Turn to **370**
To hide under the stairs?	Turn to **320**
To fight the bats?	Turn to **343**

394

The fire and the brandy warm you and you begin to feel more relaxed. You may deduct 1 *FEAR* point if you have any. You explain to the Earl what happened on the road and that you would like to use his telephone to call the local garage. 'I'm afraid our telephone line came down tonight in the storm,' he replies. 'We will have it repaired tomorrow morning. In any case, the garage would not come out here at this hour. But don't worry. You are perfectly welcome to spend the night here; I am glad of the company. Tomorrow Franklins will take you into town. Ah! Here is Franklins now.' The butler comes back in to announce that a meal is ready. You both rise to go into the dining-room. Turn to **309**.

395

The wine is impeccable; a fine vintage. Soup follows, and then you may choose either lamb (turn to **196**) or duck (turn to **115**) for your main course. Or you can tell your host that you have already eaten and you are not hungry (turn to **244**).

396

The tall cage is lowered from the wall. The back opens and you are shoved inside. It is a tight fit and you are forced up against the bars as the door is locked behind you. One of the torturer's assistants winches you up in the air. You will hang, suspended from a rope until your *STAMINA* runs out from starvation. If hunger does not take its toll quickly enough, the cramps probably will. For although you are standing up, you may not sit or lean in the cage. Your adventure is as good as over...

397

Down you fall for several metres until you finally land in a heap on something soft. Add 1 *FEAR* point for the fright and *Test your Luck*. If you are Lucky, you are unhurt. If you are Unlucky, you have twisted your wrist – deduct 1 *SKILL* point. You pick yourself up and verify there is no serious damage. You have landed on a mound of earth and hay and you realize that you are in a cellar underneath the house. The room is fairly small, with one door. Outside you can hear a shuffling noise coming closer. Will you spring behind the door to surprise whatever is approaching (turn to **6**), or will you quickly search the room for a weapon in case you need to defend yourself (turn to **355**)?

398

The stairs are very dark. You take a few steps down, trying desperately to see the stairs below you. Suddenly your foot slips and you lose your balance. Lose 3 *STAMINA* points as you tumble down the stairs, landing in a heap at the bottom. Turn to **264**.

399

Your visitor is a HUNCHBACK and he is both surprised and frightened as you leap on him. Resolve your battle:

HUNCHBACK   SKILL 7   STAMINA 7

When you have reduced his *STAMINA* to 4 points or. less, turn to **220**.

400

The creature howls as you strike the final blow. It totters on its hooves and crashes down on to the table. As it falls, its flailing arms smash into the chandelier in the centre of the room, scattering candles on to the floor. From behind you another cry goes up and your other attacker, whom you have forgotten about completely, springs over to the table to hug the beast pitifully. You ought to kill both of them; but the pathetic, sobbing creature hunched over the huge bulk is hardly worth considering. In any case, something else, much more dangerous, has caught your attention. One of the candles which was knocked from the chandelier has rolled across the floor and set light to the heavy curtains. The fire is spreading rapidly – you must escape quickly!

Smoke is beginning to creep out of the room as you close the front door behind you. Walking down the drive you glance back to see the fire making rapid progress through the ground floor. Flames are licking along the wooden beams. In an hour or so, the place will be beyond rescue. From a safe distance you watch the fire destroy the house.

A fitting end, you think, *for a house of hell.*

From a safe distance you watch the fire destroy the house

HOW TO FIGHT THE CREATURES OF THE HOUSE OF HELL

The *House of Hell* is a little different from previous Fighting Fantasy adventures. You start your adventure unarmed, with no provision or potions; *and* you have to avoid being *frightened to death!*

Before embarking on your adventure, you must first determine your own strengths and weaknesses. To see how brave, lucky and resourceful you are, you must use the dice to determine your initial *SKILL, STAMINA* and *LUCK* scores. On pages 226–227 there is an *Adventure Sheet* which you may use to record the details of an adventure. On it you will find boxes for recording your *SKILL, STAMINA* and *LUCK* scores.

You are advised either to record your scores on the *Adventure Sheet* in pencil, or, make photocopies of the page to use in future adventures.

SKILL, STAMINA AND LUCK

- Roll one die. Add 6 to this number and enter this total in the *SKILL* box on the *Adventure Sheet*. This is your

Initial SKILL. In this adventure, your Starting *SKILL* is less, because you are unarmed, but you will have the opportunity to arm yourself (see Weapons, p. 221).

- Roll both dice. Add 12 to the number rolled and enter this total in the *STAMINA* box.
- There is also a *LUCK* box. Roll one die, add 6 to this number and enter this total in the *LUCK BOX*.

For reasons that will be explained below, *SKILL, STAMINA* and *LUCK* scores change constantly during an adventure. You must keep an accurate record of these scores and for this reason you are advised either to write small in the boxes or to keep an eraser handy. But never rub out your *Initial* scores. Although you may be awarded additional *SKILL, STAMINA* and *LUCK* points, these totals may never exceed your *Initial* scores, except on very rare occasions, when you will be instructed on a particular page.

Your *SKILL* score reflects your general fighting expertize; the higher the better. Your *STAMINA* score reflects your general constitution, your will to survive, your determination and courage; the higher your *STAMINA* score, the longer you will be able to survive. Your *LUCK* score indicates how naturally lucky a person you are. Luck – and evil – are facts of life in the devilish domain you are about to explore.

BATTLES

You will often come across pages in the book which instruct you to fight ghosts, ghouls, men and beasts. An option to flee may be given, but if not – or if you choose to attack the creature anyway – you must resolve the battle as described below.

First record the creature's *SKILL* and *STAMINA* scores in the first vacant Evil Encounter Box on your *Adventure Sheet*. The scores for each creature are given in the book each time you have an encounter. The sequence of combat is then:

1. Roll both dice once for the creature. Add its *SKILL* score. This total is the creature's Attack Strength.
2. Roll both dice once for yourself. Add the number rolled to your current *SKILL* score. This total is your Attack Strength.
3. If your Attack Strength is higher than that of the creature, you have wounded it. Proceed to step 4. If the creature's Attack Strength is higher than yours, it has wounded you. Proceed to step 5. If both Attack Strength totals are the same, you have avoided each other's blows – start the next Attack Round from step 1 above.

4. You have wounded the creature, so subtract 2 points from its *STAMINA* score. You may use your *LUCK* here to do additional damage (see below).

5. The creature has wounded you, so subtract 2 points from your own *STAMINA* score. Again you may use *LUCK* at this stage (see below).

6. Make the appropriate adjustments to either the creature's or your own *STAMINA* scores (and your *LUCK* score if you used *LUCK* – see below).

7. Begin the next Attack Round by returning to your current *SKILL* score and repeating steps 1–6. This sequence continues until the *STAMINA* score of either you or the creature you are fighting has been reduced to zero (death).

FEAR

As well as surviving your adventure by ensuring that your *STAMINA* never drops to zero, in *The House of Hell* you must also avoid being *frightened to death,* Before you begin your adventure, roll one die and add 6 to the result. This total will give you the maximum *FEAR* score you can bear. Your *FEAR* score is the number of points you can take before being *frightened to death.* During your adventure, you will come across situations where you must, for example, 'Add one (or two, etc.) *FEAR* points.' Your *FEAR* score starts at zero and you must add *FEAR* points as instructed in the text. If your *FEAR* score reaches the maximum (as rolled initially – see above), then you *are frightened to death* and must end your adventure. Note that *FEAR* works in the opposite way to normal *SKILL, STAMINA* and *LUCK* scores; you start with zero and *increase* your *FEAR* score towards your maximum, rather than *subtracting,* as you do with the other scores.

ESCAPING

On some pages you may be given the option of running away from a battle should things be going badly for you. However, if you do run away, the creature automatically gets in one wound on you (subtract 2 *STAMINA* points) as you flee. Such is the price of cowardice. Note that you may use *LUCK* on this wound in the normal way (see below). You may only *Escape* if that option is specifically given to you on the page.

FIGHTING MORE THAN ONE CREATURE

If you come across more than one creature in a particular encounter, the instructions on that page will tell you how to handle the battle. Sometimes you will treat them as a single monster; sometimes you will fight each one in turn.

WEAPONS

You begin *The House of Hell* adventure with no weapon. As with other Fighting Fantasy adventures, your *SKILL* score reflects your combat ability *with* a weapon. So, before you start off on your adventure, deduct 3 points from your *SKILL* score and note this 'Starting *SKILL*'. *DO* not, however, change your *Initial SKILL,* as this is still used to determine the maximum *SKILL* you have, and is also used if you must make rolls against your *SKILL*. If you find a WEAPON (which will be identified with capital letters) during the adventure, the text will tell you how many *SKILL* points the WEAPON allows you to add. These points are added to your 'Starting *SKILL*', not your *Initial SKILL*.

LUCK

At various times during your adventure, either in battles or when you come across situations in which you could either be lucky or unlucky (details of these are given on the pages themselves), you may call on your *LUCK* to make the outcome more favourable. But beware! Using

LUCK is a risky business and if you are unlucky, the results could be disastrous.

The procedure for using your *LUCK* is as follows: roll two dice. If the number rolled is equal to or less than your current *LUCK* score, you have been lucky and the result will go in your favour. If the number rolled is higher than your current *LUCK* score, you have been unlucky and you will be penalized.

This procedure is known as *Testing your Luck*. Each time you *Test your Luck,* you must subtract one point from your current *LUCK* score. Thus you will soon realize that the more you rely on your luck, the more risky this will become.

USING LUCK IN BATTLES

On certain pages of the book you will be told to *Test your Luck* and will be told the consequences of your being lucky or unlucky. However, in battles, you always have the option of using your *LUCK* either to inflict a more serious wound on a creature you have just wounded, or to minimize the effects of a wound the creature has just inflicted on you.

If you have just wounded the creature, you may *Test your Luck* as described above. If you are lucky, you have inflicted a severe wound and may subtract an *extra 2* points from the creature's *STAMINA* score.

However, if you are unlucky, the wound was a mere graze and you must restore 1 point to the creature's *STAMINA* (i.e. instead of scoring the normal 2 points of damage, you have now scored only 1).

If the creature has just wounded you, you may *Test your Luck* to try to minimize the wound. If you are lucky, you have managed to avoid the full damage of the blow. Restore 1 point of *STAMINA* (i.e. instead of doing 2 points of damage it has done only 1). If you are unlucky, you have taken a more serious blow. Subtract 1 extra *STAMINA* point.

Remember that you must subtract 1 point from your own *LUCK* score each time you *Test your Luck*.

RESTORING SKILL, STAMINA, LUCK AND FEAR

Your *SKILL, STAMINA* and *LUCK* scores may change during your adventure. Your *SKILL* will increase (from

'Starting *SKILL*') if you find a WEAPON. Your *STAMINA* will drain as you fight creatures, and may be restored by eating or resting as instructed by the text. Your *LUCK* will run out as you must deduct one *LUCK* point each time you *Test your Luck*. Occasionally a particularly lucky find or encounter may restore some of your *LUCK*. Your *FEAR* score is built up as you go through the adventure; each time you get frightened, you will add to your *FEAR* score. Occasionally, when you get the opportunity to relax, the text may instruct you to deduct points from your *FEAR* score.

Note that any bonuses you are awarded can never be used to exceed your *Initial SKILL, STAMINA* and *LUCK* scores, nor make your *FEAR* score a minus number.

HINTS ON PLAY

There is one true way through the *House of Hell* and it will take you several attempts to find it. Make notes and draw a map as you explore – this map will be invaluable in future adventures and enable you to progress rapidly through to unexplored sections.

Remember to make a note of any advice you receive; and write down any messages or special reference numbers you are given. Some rooms are death traps and others are chambers of horror – be warned!

It will be realized that entries make no sense if read in numerical order. It is essential that you read only the entries you are instructed to read.

The one true way involves a minimum of risk and any player, no matter how weak on initial dice rolls, should be able to get through fairly easily.

May the power of good go with you!

ADVENTURE SHEET

SKILL

STAMINA

LUCK

EQUIPMENT

FEAR
(Starts at zero)

NOTES

MONSTER ENCOUNTERS

MONSTER:
SKILL =
STAMINA =

MONSTER:
SKILL =
STAMINA =

MONSTER:
SKILL =
STAMINA =

MONSTER:
SKILL =
STAMINA =

MONSTER:
SKILL =
STAMINA =

MONSTER:
SKILL =
STAMINA =

MONSTER:
SKILL =
STAMINA =

MONSTER:
SKILL =
STAMINA =

MONSTER:
SKILL =
STAMINA =

MONSTER:
SKILL =
STAMINA =

MONSTER:
SKILL =
STAMINA =

MONSTER:
SKILL =
STAMINA =

ADVENTURE SHEET

SKILL

STAMINA

LUCK

EQUIPMENT

FEAR
(Starts at zero)

NOTES

MONSTER ENCOUNTERS

MONSTER:
SKILL =
STAMINA =

MONSTER:
SKILL =
STAMINA =

MONSTER:
SKILL =
STAMINA =

MONSTER:
SKILL =
STAMINA =

MONSTER:
SKILL =
STAMINA =

MONSTER:
SKILL =
STAMINA =

MONSTER:
SKILL =
STAMINA =

MONSTER:
SKILL =
STAMINA =

MONSTER:
SKILL =
STAMINA =

MONSTER:
SKILL =
STAMINA =

MONSTER:
SKILL =
STAMINA =

MONSTER:
SKILL =
STAMINA =

YOU ARE · FIGHTING FANTASY · THE HERO

COLLECT THEM ALL, BRAVE ADVENTURER!

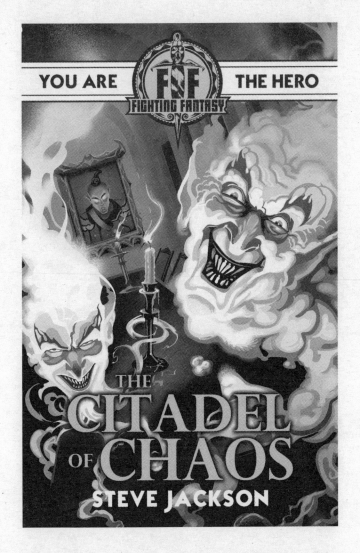

THE CITADEL OF CHAOS

STEVE JACKSON

Are YOU brave enough to enter the trap-filled lair of the
sorcerer Balthus Dire...?

You are a fearless young wizard, armed with magic spells –
the last hope to defeat the dread warlord Balthus Dire whose
sorcery threatens the land. You must enter his forbidden
citadel and take on his monstrous minions, or perish in the
process...

YOU ARE THE HERO

FIGHTING FANTASY

THE
WARLOCK
OF FIRETOP
MOUNTAIN

STEVE JACKSON & IAN LIVINGSTONE

Are YOU brave enough to take on the monsters and the magic
of Firetop Mountain?

The powerful warlock Zagor must be slain – but first you'll
need to make it through the caverns of his mountain strong-
hold. Many adventurers before you have taken a wrong turn in
the maze and perished at the hands and claws of the Warlock's
gruesome servants...

Are YOU brave enough to walk the dangerous, dark alleyways
of Port Blacksand...?

You must travel to the dark tower of demonic sorcerer Zanbar
Bone, to put an end to his reign of terror. But you'll have to
make it past the bloodthirsty thieves and creeping creatures of
the night who lurk in Port Blacksand first...

FIGHTING FANTASY

THE FOREST OF DOOM

IAN LIVINGSTONE

Are YOU brave enough to face the foes and fiends of this nightmare forest...?

A war is raging and your help is needed to vanquish the evil trolls. To save the dwarfs, you must find the grand wizard Yaztromo and track down the pieces of a legendary war hammer lost in the depths of Darkwood Forest where gruesome monsters lurk ...

YOU ARE   THE HERO

FIGHTING FANTASY

THE PORT OF PERIL

IAN LIVINGSTONE

Are YOU brave enough to face the savage demons of the underworld...?

Evil stalks the land, as undead hordes rise from their graves to terrorize the living. Embark on an epic quest from Moonstone Hills to the shadowy streets of Port Blacksand to the depths of Darkwood Forest, and ultimately face your worst nightmare...